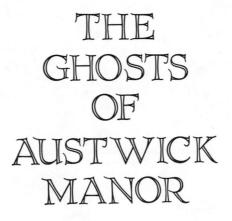

THE
GHOSTS
OF
AUSTWICK
MANOR

THE
GHOSTS
OF
AUSTWICK
MANOR

Reby Edmond MacDonald

A Margaret K. McElderry Book

ATHENEUM 1982 NEW YORK

LIBRARY OF CONGRESS CATALOGING IN PUBLICATION DATA

MacDonald, Reby Edmond
The ghosts of Austwick Manor.

"A Margaret K. McElderry book."
SUMMARY: Hillary and Heather find themselves entering
the sixteenth century as a direct result of their older
brother Don's inheritance. Will they be able
to save Don who is in grave danger from an ancient curse?
[1. Mystery and detective stories.
2. Space and time—Fiction] I. Title.
PZ7.E2437Gh   [Fic]   81-10779
ISBN 0-689-50212-5   AACR2

Published simultaneously in Canada
by McClelland & Stewart, Ltd.
Composed by American–Stratford Graphic Services, Inc.
Brattleboro, Vermont
Manufactured by Fairfield Graphics
Fairfield, Pennsylvania
Designed by Felicia Bond
First Edition

*For the Young of the MacDonald clan
who are weary
of
"E-I! E-I! O!"
and would like to exchange
the old farm
for
a Tudor manor
complete with ghosts*

THE
GHOSTS
OF
AUSTWICK
MANOR

_⌒_ *CHAPTER ONE*

WE WERE HAVING BREAKFAST IN A PATCH OF THIN morning sunlight when Father brought in the mail. He sorted through it as Mother poured the coffee and grunted as he tossed each piece down. "Nothing but junk ads and bills—except one and it's addressed to you, Mary," he said and passed it across to Mother. She put down the percolator and examined it curiously. I should say right here that we all call George Stanton "Father," although he is really our stepfather. Perhaps my brother Don is able to remember our own father, but I can't— well, I don't think I can really—and Heather was only a baby when he had the accident.

Mother read the address on the envelope out loud and smiled. "Mrs. George V. Stanton and Master Donald MacDonald."

My fifteen-year-old brother stopped spooning out strawberry jam and said, "Who?"

Heather let out a whoop and cried, *"Master! Master Donald!"* and kept it up until Don yelled, "Pipe down!" in such a voice that she was squelched and had to grin and enjoy it in silence as the rest of us were doing.

"It's possibly a prospectus from another summer

camp," said Father. "The quality of their stationery gets better every year."

Meanwhile, my mother was trying to slit the envelope. She was very pregnant and couldn't even handle the envelope and the knife easily without her elbow bumping into her stomach. She couldn't get too close to the table, either. "No, it's from a London barrister," she said in surprise. "But he has crossed out the English address and has written under it the date and Empress Hotel, Victoria, B.C.—so he must be in town."

"What's a barrister?" demanded Heather.

"A kind of lawyer," I said.

"What's his name?" asked Father.

Mother's eyes flicked to the bottom of the page. "Jason X. Willoughby."

Our breakfast was forgotten. She began to read.

> *"Dear Mrs. Stanton:*
>
> *Your late husband's great-uncle, Donald MacDonald, when he heard I had business in Vancouver, asked me if I would extend my trip as far as Vancouver Island and call on his heir, your son—also bearing the ancient name—who will become the head of this branch of the family in due course. At this point, I must warn you against any great expectations—death duties have wasted the family fortune long since. However, there are several items that he desires Master Donald to take charge of—mostly family records, a portrait, et cetera, et cetera. My client is very anxious about the future of these things and desires me to meet Master*

Donald and explain the importance of them.
If all is satisfactory, they will be delivered to
him anon. Therefore, will you call the hotel
and inform me when it would be convenient
to wait on you for this purpose? I shall make
no plans to return to England until I hear
from you,

> *Sincerely,*
> *Jason X. Willoughby"*

There was a long silence, then Heather demanded indignantly, "What does he mean 'head of the family'? Don's only fifteen!"

"I have no idea," said Mother.

"It's all some kind of a joke," said Don shortly.

Father smiled. "I wouldn't mind if someone played such a joke on me."

"It seems he's come to the Island just to see you, Don, so we'd better do as he says. Will you call the hotel, George?"

But Father was looking at Don. "Don should call."

"Not I!" said my brother starting on the strawberry jam again.

"If you're old enough to receive letters from a London barrister, you're certainly old enough to arrange a meeting. Anything else is sophomoric," said Father.

Heather punched me under the table. "What's that mean, Hillary?"

"It means young, gauche, like a sophomore in school, I think."

Don glared at me, then threw his napkin down and made for the hall where the telephone was. I saw Father glance at Mother and wink.

5

After a few minutes, Don returned. He looked quite satisfied with himself. "Mr. Willoughby will call here tomorrow evening at eight," he said. "I offered the car, but he prefers to come by taxi."

"Well done," said Father. "It's much better to act than stew about things," and he kissed our mother and went off to the university.

The next evening, as eight o'clock approached, the family assembled in front of the fireplace. Heather and I wanted to dress up, but Mother said our tidiest school sweaters and skirts would do—after all, Mr. Willoughby wasn't coming to meet *us*, but to instruct Don about his duties as "Keeper of the Family Records and et cetera, et cetera." She laughed as she said it. "It's all very old-world and charming, girls—but not terribly important. So just relax."

Father continued to read the paper, although I noticed that he had got out the best sherry, and Don himself came down only at the last minute looking unconcerned and asked to see the sports page.

Precisely on the hour a taxi drove up. We weren't allowed to peek. Our father went to greet our visitor and we heard voices in the hall as he took his hat and coat. Then the sitting room door opened and he brought in an elderly gentleman.

Mr. Willoughby was bony. The skin was stretched over his skull tightly so that you could see veins like blue worms lying just below the surface. His flesh was like oiled paper with freckles. He was dressed in tweeds so hairy you could have shaved them and he had a cane with a gold bulldog's head for a knob although he didn't seem lame. I think he used it as a pointer, like the principal at our school—or a weapon.

We came to our feet to meet him. Father introduced us. "My wife, Mary Stanton, her daughters, Miss Hillary MacDonald and Miss Heather, and this is—"

The old man turned to Don and smiled, showing teeth the color of mastodon ivory. "So this is MacDonald's heir!" he exclaimed and shook hands with my brother. Later, Don said it was like having his fingers crunched by a handful of chicken bones.

Mr. Willoughby was still looking at my brother keenly. "Yes, you have the lean greyhound look, my lad. It's in the portraits for centuries past—the thin, hooked nose, the scroll of the ear and the long hands—and I daresay the long feet to go with them, eh? Ha! Ha!" His laugh was like the rustle of dry leaves.

Don could say nothing to all this. He was blushing. We tried not to look at him and we all smiled politely. Heather just stared at the gold bulldog on the cane.

"Shall we sit down?" said Mother and led us girls to the couch to sit beside her.

My father indicated a comfortable chair for Mr. Willoughby and found one for himself. Don was about to choose a seat as far from the company as possible when the visitor tapped a straight chair near his and commanded, "Sit here, my lad." Don abandoned his refuge and obediently took the one facing the old man.

"May I pour you a glass of sherry, sir?" Father asked.

"Later, thank you, Mr. Stanton. Later. . . . Now," he said fixing Don with a stern eye, "what do you know of your father's great-uncle MacDonald?"

Don shot a quick glance at Mother for help, got none and said, "Nothing, sir."

The old man made a tut-tutting noise and himself

7

turned to Mother almost accusingly. She said quickly, "My late husband didn't speak of his family very often. I sensed he was at odds with them. If he ever mentioned a great-uncle, I don't remember it."

"Yes, yes," Mr. Wiloughby said impatiently, "Mr. Donald quarreled with a cousin and left the country, but he shouldn't have cut his children off from their heritage because of a foolish disagreement."

"His children were very young when he was killed," she pointed out reasonably. "Don was only seven, Hillary was four and Heather, a baby—hardly the ages to absorb family history."

"So it seems I must begin at the beginning." Mr. Willoughby sighed and seemed to collect his strength. Then he turned his gaze on Don. After a minute he stated almost accusingly, "You come from an ancient family, lad."

As he seemed to be waiting for a reply, my brother muttered, "Yes sir. The Massacre of Glencoe, the Lords of the Isles and the Battle of Cullodon."

"Oh, we're not concerned with Highland history," our visitor said impatiently. "No, no! In the mid-sixteenth century there was a MacDonald at the English court. Cast your mind back to the sixteenth century." We could all see Don casting his mind back and bringing up nothing at all. "To the court of Mary Tudor?" nudged Mr. Willoughby fiercely and waited. He was acting just like a teacher Don and I each had had at different times who terrorized history classes. I saw that my brother was thinking of him now; that teacher had given us both sweaty palms.

"Bloody Mary?" said Don uncertainly.

Mr. Willoughby threw up his hands. "It's a good

thing Mr. MacDonald isn't with us to hear you say that!" Don looked more nervous than ever. I was nervous too, in sympathy. Our visitor went on: "Now listen carefully, my lad! Your ancestor of that date did a service for Mary when she was still a princess and was rewarded in 1540 with lands and a handsome house called Austwick Manor. This noble lady, who suffered so much at the hands of her father, old Henry the Eighth, was grateful to the Scot and honored him mightily. When her very own father called her 'bastard,' everyone shunned her, —was afraid to befriend her." (Heather was listening to this part of the story with interest.) "But MacDonald served this lonely girl and when she came to the throne in 1553, she remembered, bless her, and heaped further honors on him. It was the beginning of your family's eminence, my lad. Later of course, the MacDonald fortunes ebbed and flowed with the various successions. They fell under Elizabeth, rose under James, rose higher still under Charles and were almost annhilated under Cromwell—that warthog of the people!" Here he stopped and seemed to have trouble getting control of himself. He finally lifted his head and stared around almost savagely. "It's sad to think that what Cromwell didn't finish off, the modern British government did with death duties and taxes. It's all gone, my lad—all! My client, the present head of the family, has lived in lodgings for years—lived out of a trunk, with a few bulky possessions in storage. He is now eighty-five years old and anxious to get the family affairs in order."

My mother said sympathetically, "Is Mr. MacDonald ill, then?"

"Not at all, ma'am. But he realizes he can't last much longer. Your son is next in line now that his father predeceased him. He wants to know if this lad will do to take over. Well, Donald?"

Don looked at him blankly. When he looks like this people wonder about him. Heather has the same trick. But he's thinking and taking his time about it. Mr. Willoughby began to look a little exasperated at his lack of response. My brother finally spoke. "Would my father have taken it on?"

"Certainly—no question!"

"If I don't, who's next in line for the job?"

"There's a regrettable second cousin—plays a guitar in a band in Soho, I believe—on the move all the time. Can't see him taking charge of family papers and the et ceteras. Besides, he's not in line. It would be the end, the end of a family with a noble place in history. Oliver would dance in his dirty shroud."

"Oliver?"

"Cromwell, of course."

"Oh." Don looked across at Heather and me. "There are two other MacDonalds in the room," he said. "I'd like to know what they think."

I said eagerly, "Of course you must do it, Don!"

Heather said, "Why not? But I don't know that I see you as the head of—" I kicked her and she grunted and shut up.

Mr. Willoughby made a courtly bow in our direction. "While it isn't customary to seek out the opinion of the female members of the family, they've no doubt always had a big say behind the scenes," he said and smiled.

I didn't care for that too much and I saw my mother staring at him too, but as she was the hostess, I knew

10

she'd let it pass. Heather, however, turned to her and whispered, "Isn't that male—?"

"Shh," said Mother.

"So that's settled," Mr. Willoughby said slapping his knee. "Now I'll have that sherry you offered, Mr. Stanton, and we'll drink to it."

We all got a taste of the sherry and a chance to clink glasses, which is always fun, although you have to watch Heather because she's inclined to go at things too hard; then Father got his coat and prepared to drive our visitor back to the Empress Hotel.

As he was leaving Mr. Willoughby went to Mother and took her hand. "When is the happy event to be?" he asked.

"Second week in April," she said.

"Splendid! Splendid! I suppose you're hoping to balance your little family, two boys and two girls?"

Heather who hardly ever spoke up in strange company blurted out, "We've had tests! We know it's going to be a girl. We're going to call her Rebecca."

Mr. Willoughby looked surprised. "Tests?" he said.

"That's true," said Mother smiling. "It's going to be a girl."

"Science! It takes all the fun and surprise out of things!" He shook his bony head. But now he was looking at Heather. Suddenly he stooped down and peered at her. "How old are you, Mistress Heather?" he asked.

My sister's eyebrows shot up but she contained herself and said, "Eight and a half, sir."

"Are you fond of dollhouses?" he asked.

"Not much," she said. "Mostly I like to skate with my friends Christy and Nikki."

11

"Good, good!" he grunted straightening up. "Then you won't be tempted."

He didn't ask me how old I was or anything at all, but I'm used to not being noticed. Being the middle child is no fun.

When Father got back from the hotel later, he was laughing. "What an extraordinary old man!" he said. "He told me to get Don interested in history and was most insistent. We are also to nurture a sense of responsibility in him toward his family, and we can expect to receive the items quite soon—a few packing cases right out of storage in London. He said he was glad we had a roomy house and he said he'd give a good report to old Mr. MacDonald when he got back."

"A *few* packing cases?" said mother doubtfully. "The house is not that roomy! You'll have to keep the stuff in your room, Don, or in the basement."

But I was curious. "Why did our father quarrel with the family, Mother?" I asked. "I'd like to know about that."

"We didn't talk about it, dear. I remember he once said they were a superstitious lot and he was fed up with them."

"Were they uneducated?" I asked.

"Not at all. Superstition raises its head in the most unlikely places. My own mother wouldn't wear green or open an umbrella in the house, and she always threw salt over her shoulder when she spilled it—although she would walk under a ladder. Still, it hardly seems anything to quarrel over, does it? Rather more something to laugh at."

I was thinking that there must have been something else. I could see that Don thought so too.

Meanwhile, Heather made herself a nuisance to Don, demanding that he let her examine the "long family nose and the scroll of his ear." She admired his "long fingers" and crawled around on the rug to glimpse his "even longer feet," until he rolled her over in a fury and stamped out of the room. At which point Heather wailed in mock dramatic tones, "Oh dear, the Head of our Family is mad at me! What shall I do! Save me! Save me, sister mine!" and clung to me.

Even Mother had trouble controlling her. "Of course it's sibling rivalry," she said to the rest of us. But Heather, who had caught the ghost of a smile on Father's face, got carried away. She wailed and flapped around and cried, "Pity me, noble Scot!—a poor little bastard am I!—a poor, bloody little bastard you see before you! Save me and I shall give you titles and honors!"

Father moved fast. He picked her up bodily and carried her up to our room. We heard him say above Heather's protests, "Enough! Your brother is being called on to do a man's job for his family, and I'll not have you make light of it! Stop it this instant!"

That evening the house was heavy, with no one talking much. We all knew Heather was feeling badly done to. But it was true that she couldn't bear all that attention being given to someone other than herself— especially as people always went on about how cute and freckled and pigtailed she was. You would never know that she was really very fond of Don, but she was.

People are strange.

13

⌒ CHAPTER TWO

WHEN THREE MONTHS OR MORE HAD PASSED AND Mr. Willoughby had almost slipped from our minds, Don received notice that said: "Dear Sir: A shipment consigned to you has arrived and is awaiting you at Outer Wharf. Please claim same as soon as possible." It had come by sea, via the Panama Canal.

He went off with Father pulling a small U-Haul and returned a few hours later pulling a much larger one, and it was loaded high and the springs creaked.

"When we saw what there was, we had to exchange the trailer for a bigger one," he said.

Heather and I stood with Mother at the curb and stared. The trailer was stacked with cases! They were so heavy that we had to ask neighbors to help get them unloaded and then borrow a dolly to roll them to the steps and get them up on the porch. There was one very flat picture crate and several smaller sturdy ones the size of footlockers labeled "USED BOOKS," and there was one enormous one that was big enough to contain a refrigerator—a big, double commercial refrigerator, and it took all of us pushing and shoving to get it into place on the porch. This one was labeled "TOYS" and "THIS END UP"

14

and "FRAGILE!" in a dozen places. Heather let out a whoop of excitement, but Mother looked dismayed and Don apologetic. Father looked puzzled and a little amused.

They decided to open the cases on the porch to save mess. The plan was to attack the small ones first and get them out of the way so we could have room to move around the big one. So Don brought a short crowbar and pried a cover up on the nearest one and we looked down on a tight row of ancient journals with dates on the spines that we could hardly believe. The writing was so strange that we couldn't make it out but Father read off, "Household Accounts, 1540–41" and so on in sequence. There were about twelve of these big books to a crate and there were about ten crates. Don and Father stared at the old, decaying volumes. What to do with them?

"I think you'll have to take them into your room, Don. Just set up the crates as they are. Stack them like shelves."

So the cases were hauled up to Don's room and stacked against the wall one on top of the other, and suddenly he had a wall of books. Then Heather tugged at Father and cried, "Now the toys!"

We trooped back down to the porch. Father took up one tool and Don another and they applied them to both ends of the lid and the nails squealed and resisted and then gave way. Heather was dancing in glee as they laid it aside, but the contents were still thoroughly padded. On top was a sheet of notepaper and a message in bold letters stared up at them. "IMPORTANT! READ THIS BEFORE PROCEEDING FURTHER!"

"It's all yours, Don," Father said.

Don picked up the paper gingerly, unfolded it and read out: " 'THIS IS NOT A TOY! That label was a shipping convenience only! This is a family treasure! It is a model of our ancient home, Austwick Manor, faithfully rendered to the last portrait on the wall. However, it is only of the front section. The house had two great wings that went back from each end. The large, square court was made complete by a set of stables across the rear. It was also moated. This exquisite model was built in 1552–1553 for a beloved daughter who had married in a distant country. It took one year to fabricate and longer for artisans to make copies of the furnishings. It is a perfect example of a moated Tudor house of that period and from it we can see how people lived at that time. It must be carefully assembled, then locked up and preserved for future members of our family. This is your responsibility, Donald! No item must be toyed with or lost. I trust to you the only remaining treasure of our family—the one object of value that did not go to the block to be sold for death duties. Everything else has gone. God be with you, my boy.' "

It was signed "D. MacDonald," and then there was a postscript. "Our old home has been in storage for so long, how happy it will be to see the light of day again! But you must observe all directions carefully. They have been worked out over the centuries and are *best!* If you do, all will be well. This is a warning! Take it! D. MacD."

A long silence followed this strange message. Even Heather was quiet.

"Well," said Mother at last. "I don't know what to think! It looks rather too big to live with, but then it sounds intriguing, so let's take a look at it." I thought

16

her eyes gleamed as she said this. I know she liked doll-houses. She had made me one once out of an orange crate and had spent hours decorating it.

Father and Don pried off the front of the case and it took all of us to ease out the blanketed shape inside. Under it we found a separate stand, a splendid piece of furniture slightly higher than a coffee table. It was oak with twisted legs, and it was very old and very hand-some. Mother now decided it would have to stand in the bay window of the dining room, for it was much too big for Don's room—besides the traffic was not as great there.

And so Don carried in the heavy stand, and we un-wrapped the padded blanket from the model house and staggered in with it and set it on its stand. Then we stood back and looked at it. It was a Tudor house of half-timber and brick construction. It had small, diamond-paned casements and an imposing entrance with a coat of arms over the door. Stone leopards guarded the steps and the front door was massive and studded with iron knobs. What was surprising was that the lower left front corner was a chapel and the entrance to that was a smaller arched door on the end. The model was built on a base about fifteen inches deep and at the right hand end of this was a drawer, narrow and deep, which went from front to back. Don pulled it open. Here, we found another note lying on top of a pile of wadding. "These dolls represent some of the inmates of the house begin-ning about 1550. Do not handle them. They are fragile. Leave them in the drawer! This is a warning. D. MacD."

My brother lifted up the padding, and we stared down at the row of little figures dressed in silks and satins, in linen, leather and furs; the lord of the manor and his lady, his family and his servants, their faces all

17

embroidered on fine, handwoven linen, their hair and beards of lamb's wool or even human hair. Heather fell to her knees beside the drawer blocking all our vision.

Don was anxious. "It says, 'Don't touch them.' "

"Is it all right if I breathe on them?"

"Don't be smart," said Father. "Don is right. They're not meant to be played with."

I went around to peer through the windows. The rooms were packed tightly with boxes of all sizes, but I glimpsed walls that were paneled or plastered and ceilings that were beamed or painted. Through the chapel windows I saw memorial brass plates sct in stone walls and in the floor. On each side of the plain altar lay knights carved in stone and their ladies. In the packing case there had been many boxes packed in between the legs of the stand, all labeled, and now we carried them to our dining room table and piled them up. It was like getting ready to decorate the Christmas tree.

Father found that the model opened up across the front in two leaves and at the back, also. These were held shut by small iron padlocks and keys were tied to the locks. He opened them one by one. "O.K., Don, take over," he said.

Don hesitated, then began drawing out the boxes. He became a little edgy because the rest of us couldn't resist lifting the lids and peeking in. We glimpsed small furniture, glassware, folded draperies and linen and portraits, all properly packed in tiny cases, while Don fretted at us. At last the house was emptied and reduced to a shell and our dining table was stacked high with labeled boxes.

Don now stared at the house helplessly, but when we put out a hand to touch it, he fussed and hovered and warned us off. He got us as flustered as he was. He was infuriating.

Mother spoke to him quietly and reasonably with her hands at her side—to show she was no threat, I suppose. "It has to be set up. Do you want to do it all yourself?—because it's going to be quite a job."

"Well. . . ." he said. "Well, you can help, I guess. But not the girls. It's not a toy." And he repeated it fiercely, glaring at us, "It's not a toy!"

Heather looked sulky, but she kept her hands off, as Mother and I were doing, but I knew the strain she was under, because I was, too. Father, meanwhile, was crawling on his hands and knees around the base. "All pegged together!" he explained. "Extraordinary cabinetwork!"

"Do you want to make a start?" Mother asked Don calmly.

He nodded, but continued to stare at it helplessly, so she walked over to the dining table and looked over the boxes. They were old and of all shapes and sizes and each had a label pasted on the end that said in bold, black ink words like "Master Bed Chamber," or "Kitchen," "Stillroom," "Attic." She chose two labeled "Great Hall" and opened them while Heather and I pushed in eagerly to see. Don couldn't stop us from just looking. In each box was a floor plan, showing where each piece should be placed and where each picture hung. One of these papers said, "No variations!" She smoothed out the paper and handed it to me and said, "Well now . . . !" and lifted from the box a massive refectory table and chairs and a court cupboard. "Pictures first, I think. . . . Which wall, Hillary? You have the plan."

"That's the one from over the fireplace," I said. "The Girl in Blue goes on the side wall, the tapestry on the inside wall."

Mother handled it carefully; she put her hand into the cavity of the great hall and got the things placed.

Heather picked up a small chair to hand it to her and Don yelled and flapped at her like a bad-tempered goose in a farmyard and almost made her drop it. We both glared at him. Heather, shaken, stamped her foot and yelled, "You can keep your darned old dollhouse!" and stormed out. He was lucky she didn't throw the little chair at him.

The rest of us continued the job in heavy silence; I read from the plans and Mother placed the pieces.

"That narrow drawer at the end with the dolls— now why is there just one of them? There's room in the base for six more like it. Father said. What do you think, Don?"

My brother seemed relieved to be called on to consider problems of structure and went down on his knees beside Father to puzzle over it.

The base was pretend stone—gesso, my father said. Every six inches or so, there was one carved block. Don was rapping on the base with his knuckles to see if it sounded hollow when he hit the front carving and a ten-inch portion swung out. They both yelled in surprise. We saw a small, stone-lined room and in the walls were iron rings that I didn't much like the look of. There was an arched wooden door through the interior wall that led to somewhere beyond.

"There must be a matching space at the back," said Father, and Don went around to look. He pressed a knob there under the stillroom and a similar flap opened, disclosing a wine cellar.

Don was excited now. "There's got to be more room under the great hall and the chapel!" he said and he crawled around to the end of the house and pressed the center there. A flap immediately flew open and we all stared at another enclosure, much larger than the others —as large as the chapel and room above combined. It was arched, and there were deep shelves cut into the walls. There was a stone table in the center of the floor and nothing else.

Father said, "Why, it's the family crypt!"

"And they lived over it?" Mother said in surprise.

"I think I saw a box." said Don, and he hurried over to the pile and brought one back. He lifted off the lid and passed the paper of the floor plan to Father, then he began to lift out small coffins—each with a brass name plate. Father read off names and dates and the inscriptions, all in Latin. "I imagine everyone's accounted for here, if we only knew it," he said quietly when he had finished.

Mother shivered. Don began to slip them into the proper niches in the wall. Heather had returned, unable to resist our shout of discovery. Her eyes were red-rimmed and she was silent, but she stood quietly and stared with the rest of us as the small coffins were sorted and put in their proper shelves according to the plan. We knew she was there, and we pretended she had never been away.

We were all quieter now as we went back to arranging the upper rooms. "My hands are so clumsy," grumbled Mother, "I set up one thing and knock down two.

This job takes smaller fingers than I have. Heather, I think you're the only one who can reach in and set up those silver trenchers against the wall there."

We all glanced at Don. He said nothing. Heather, with a sideways look at him, took the piece of silver almost covertly and reached in daintily and got it propped up on the side table and Mother then passed her the Venetian glass goblets and all the other tiny, delicate things. "That's good, dear," Mother said. "I'm sure I'd have broken something."

I stood to one side brooding a little, thinking how Heather almost always got her way, when Mother said, "The great bed has to be made up, Hillary. You're much better at folding things than I am—it's all that Origami you've practiced. If you make it up out here, we can slip it into place when it's ready."

I jumped to attention. I took the small sheets that were no bigger than a handkerchief and the bed hangings and coverlet, which were all embroidered in colored wool, and I made it up. It had a feather bed and as fast as I got one sheet on neatly, a dimple appeared in it and I had to plump it up again—which is how I discovered feather beds are a pain! While I did this, Mother found a "one-holer" with a velvet padded seat which made us all laugh.

Meanwhile, Don and Father were busy setting up the wine cellar with its kegs and barrels, and the dungeon. Nothing much went into it but two buckets and some gray blankets and an iron brazier and a cot with rope for slats. Then they puzzled over the mechanics of the roasting jack and its mass of wheels and chains and pulleys in the kitchen, and I got to place the tiny mouse by the mousehole.

22

Don did the attic himself. Very strange things were stored up there: iron-bound chests, rusty chain mail—even armor for a horse. The facepiece had a long spike in the center of the forehead. The horse must have looked like a unicorn; it would have been terrifying to meet head on. If a knight's lance didn't impale you, his horse's iron horn just might. There were chests of silks and "foot warmers" to hold burning charcoal to put in the carriage on freezing days. There was also an old wooden saddle with remnants of red velvet still attached and parts of some unused bedsteads and bird cages. I wish we had an attic like that!

Father found a box labeled "Priest Hole," which contained a cot, a small praying stool and a long oak bench. Then the search was on for this secret place. Don found it by noting that the chimney stack was bigger in the attic than in the lower rooms. They measured again, and sure enough, found a long narrow room behind the false front of the attic chimney. This brick wall swung out and Father put the bits of furniture in it and rolled the section back.

"Why would anyone hide in there?" Heather asked, puzzled, as she watched the odd-shaped room disappear and become just a wide chimney again.

"Because people were after him," Don said.

"Who?"

"Different people at different times, depending on who was in power on the throne. It was a nasty age when they chopped off people's heads or burned them at the stake."

"Don . . .!" Mother murmured. Heather looked interested.

"Well it was," said Don. "That's history."

Father dearly loved the theater. He saw every New York show that came to town. He helped produce the plays the college put on—Shakespeare, even. It was his hobby. He looked at the model of the Elizabethan house and his eyes glowed. "It needs the costumed figures to set it off," he said. "What do you think, Don?"

Don was alarmed. "It said not to touch them! They're fragile!"

"What's the difference if a doll lies in the drawer or lies on a bed—and no one will be handling them."

"I know, but it said not to—!"

"It'll look great, Don!" cried Heather, quite recovered from her tears.

"And it will be locked up, of course," said Father.

"Well . . . I guess, if you don't handle them too much. . . . I suppose the materials are all rotted by time," Don said still doubtfully.

We gathered around the deep drawer and peered down at the small dolls. Just then the telephone shrilled. Don went to answer it. We heard him cry, "Oh, I clean forgot! Sorry! No, family business! All right, Coach. I'll come right away!" He stuck his head around the door. "I forgot the soccer game!"

"But we haven't opened the picture crate yet!" Mother called. "The large picture crate!"

"I have to go!"

"OK. Run along. We'll finish up here," Father said.

We heard Don seize his kit and rush out the door. He mounted his bicycle at the gate and pedaled off fast. I couldn't imagine how he could leave all the excitement here, but he did.

"Well," said Mother. "Let's see. Who shall we set up?"

We looked at the little figures again. We saw now that under the papers of warning there was a small tag with dates. The top layer said 1550; and under that was another row of dolls dated half a century later, and under that more, each group in a different style of dress.

"We need the parents," said Heather.

"The cook," Father said and laughed.

"The girl in the blue velvet dress," I chimed in.

"We'll put out the first set, the oldest," said Mother, and she lifted out the gentleman of the house. He wore a long gown of rich patterned material and over it an equally long velvet coat with great sleeves. He had a red beard and his hair was to his shoulders. If he had the high hooked nose that Mr. Willoughby spoke about you couldn't see it on his linen-flat face. "Where shall we put him?" she asked.

"At his writing desk in the great chamber."

Mother set him down carefully in the heavy oaken chair, and he leaned forward as if he were studying what he was going to write. She picked up the mother next, a splendid figure in very complicated clothes with her hair in a jeweled net and over it a little hat wired stiffly and with veiling hanging down the rear. Mother sat her down in the same room by the fireplace in front of her embroidery frame.

I pointed to the girl doll in a sapphire blue velvet dress with a high-standing lace collar and Mother took her up carefully and set her into the second chamber and gave her the lute.

The cook in a big apron was put on a stool by the fireplace to stir a black pot, and there was a maid in the stillroom where she could go on with her work of distilling toilet water and cough syrups and making liniments and poultices and soap. That was Mother's suggestion. The priest sat in the attic reading, ready to dive behind the chimney if he had to, and there was a sturdy character in a leather apron who was at the back door. "He's come from the stables and is asking for a tankard of ale," said Father. Our parents were having as much fun as we were with the house. Heather and I looked at them and then at each other and giggled.

Heather went back to the drawer. There was just one doll left in the top row, a ragged, unkempt man with long, shaggy hair. Even though his eyes were only embroidered on his linen face with black thread, they stared up at us villainously. He had a smudged spot on his brow, which didn't help his appearance, but I couldn't tell whether it was meant to be there or was just a rust mark on the old linen. His gown was tattered and his feet below the torn hem were in sandals.

"I think I know where he goes," said Father and placed him in the dungeon.

"Oh dear . . . !" said Mother. "Let's leave this one in the drawer. I don't like him at all!"

Father laughed. "If it's a true model of the year 1550 everything must be in place the way it was." So he put the doll on the cot with the gray blankets and the battered plate and the iron basket on legs that was the brazier. Then he closed all the sections and snapped the four small padlocks shut.

Mother went off to prepare dinner then and Father wandered off to Don's room to take down the first volume of the Household Accounts and the Journal dated 1540 and began to puzzle out the strange and difficult script.

Heather and I dusted all the outside windowsills

with a feather and patted the leopards beside the stone steps and hummed as we worked. We had to imagine the moat; I wondered what it was like—how wide it had been and if you could put a boat on it—and did it have a bridge over it. It would have had to be one that could be defended, I guessed.

"I wish it was mine!" Heather said. Well, I wished it was mine!—so I didn't say anything to that. "You're already too old, Hil," she confided. "You're twelve. But I could really use it." I said nothing and let her maunder on. "It's just right for me. . . . Oh, why do boys always have to be the head of the family anyway, and inherit things! Why not girls?"

"Oh, they can today. But even if they can, it wouldn't go to you because I'm next in line. I'm older than you are."

She sighed. "I just hate being the youngest! It isn't fair!"

"You won't be for long," I said, thinking about the new baby. Of course, this one would have a different father. This one would be our stepfather's child. It wouldn't be a MacDonald as we were—just the same, we were very excited about it and looking forward to having Rebecca—even if we had to share our room. Heather was silent thinking about it. . . . Anyway, I thought it awful being the middle child. I thought Heather had it easy!

That night Heather dreamed of the house. I heard her muttering about it in her sleep. I called across to the other bed. "You awake?"

Her voice came from the darkness. "I can't sleep!"

"Neither can I."

"I haven't slept at all!"

She had, of course, because she'd been dreaming out loud. "Let's get some milk," I said.

We put on our silk-padded dressing gowns that our grandmother Bruin had sent us—Heather's daffodil yellow, mine red as Christmas—which always made us feel sleek and silky, and tiptoed down to the kitchen. We found the cookies and a box of crackers and some cheese and, with the glasses on a tray, took it all into the dining room to be near the house.

The model was in the big alcove formed by the bay, and the moonlight shone through our own high windows and then through the diamond panes of the model. With only a distant light in the kitchen to take away the scariness of midnight, we sat in the gloom quietly, our plates beside us, and marveled at how real it looked. It was as if the house was lit up in every room. Heather breathed, "Isn't it wonderful, Hil?"

I nodded. From the distant boulevard came an occasional roar of a deisel truck, and from our own street the car lights of a late homecomer would flit by and light the bay brightly for a second or two. Once our neighbor's standard poodle, Muffin, barked and was answered by the black dog, Cerberus, who lived down at the corner. The small rooms seemed to come alive from the passing lights, the objects within casting shadows of their own. The effect was eerie.

Heather whispered, "Oh, Hil, I saw something move!"

A strange feeling went up my backbone like fizzing soda water, and I champed up my last cookie without even noticing I'd eaten it. "It's just the tree bobbing in front of the streetlight that's flicking shadows at us. . . ."

"No," she said. "I saw the girl doll move!"

CHAPTER THREE

IT WAS STRANGE SITTING IN THE GLOOM WITH THE night sounds drifting in to us and the moving shadows. I said, keeping my voice even, "The doll in the blue dress? Maybe it fell over. Let's look."

But before I could slide off my chair to investigate, new and different sounds came to my ears, a great jingling of harness and the clop of many hooves, the creaking of wheels and muted voices calling out orders. I saw the glow of lanterns and the fiercer smoky flames of torches, and a cavalcade of mounted men and many carriages swept up a great driveway and came to a jangling stop at the bridge that spanned the moat—yes! I saw a bridge. The house stood in a wooded park that was flooded by moonlight. Beyond the bridge, the front door opened and a stately woman in a cloak stepped out, followed by a crowd of others also dressed for traveling. A tall, powerful-looking man knelt and kissed her hand; his woman moved forward and kissed the lady's hand also. A younger girl curtsied deeply, sinking into the folds of her padded dress, and there were younger children too, and they all bobbed. Then the noble lady crossed the bridge, was handed into the first carriage, and her friends into theirs, and the doors clicked shut right along the line. The torches guttered and flared before and behind the coaches. Someone shouted, and the horses leaned into their harness and they all swept away down the drive between the trees with the torches streaming fire. For a few moments the people of the house stood on the bridge waving, then they walked back and the heavy iron-bound door closed behind them leaving the stone leopards alone in the cold moonlight.

I had watched all this with my heart pounding. I dared not speak. I didn't know if it had really happened or if I'd imagined it. I looked sideways at Heather just as she moved closer to me and put her hand in mine. It was icy cold.

"Did you see anything?" she whispered.

"I thought I saw people," I answered, "but of course, that's crazy."

"But I really did, Hil!"

"What did you see?"

"People driving away and other people waving!"

I didn't want to admit to anything, it would frighten her too much. Mother says that, while Heather is the feistiest one of the family, she is really highly strung and we must try to keep her calm. She's younger and we have to remember that, too. So I said, "It must be just a trick of the lights. Let's look, then you'll see they're all in their places." But I was just as frightened as she was as I made myself move forward.

But suddenly our dining room carpet was crunching with the sound of gravel, and we were crossing the drive where there was none before and then crossing the bridge over the moat. We mounted the few steps between the leopards and opened the iron-studded door with its great knocker. And we weren't frightened at all! We closed it behind us and moved quietly toward a grand wooden staircase. It didn't seem at all odd. Courage wasn't even called for. We simply went up the wide stairs, which we seemed to know well. It had another leopard for a newel post and Heather patted it on its polished rump as she went past as if she were used to it. The walls of the stairwell were hung with portraits, and there was a suit of armor at the half-landing. Two doors faced each other across the top landing—the great chamber and the small chamber. We turned toward the smaller one and knocked gently.

Someone was sobbing inside. I was sure our knock couldn't be heard over it, so I turned the knob and we went in. We were in a small, oak-paneled room with a fireplace. There was a table near the window covered with books and a lute beside a chair. The girl in the blue dress was lying across her goose-feather bed and it billowed around her like risen bread. (And I'd had such a time plumping it up!) She was crying bitterly.

I said loudly, "What's the trouble? Can we help?"

The girl sat up startled and looked at us from between the damask curtains. She was about fifteen. Her eyes were red, her beautiful wired lace collar crushed, and the silk velvet of her blue dress was pulled up enough to show a velvet slipper with flowers embroidered on the toes.

"Who are you?" She hiccoughed. "Did you come with the princess? Have they left without you?"

"No. . . ." I started to say, but she interrupted.

"Oh, you're part of that troupe of montebanks that entertained us. What are you doing in this part of the house? They fed you in the kitchen, didn't they?"

"What makes you think we're part of a troupe?" I asked, hurt.

"Your costumes. What are you supposed to be?"

I looked down at myself. My grandmother likes to make our nightclothes and they look nice. Under our padded dressing gowns, we each wore a long flannel nighty with a small frill of the same material around the throat and wrist.

With dignity I said, "I'm Hillary MacDonald and this is my sister, Heather." Heather, as usual with someone strange, was silent and just stared.

"Oh, more of the family," the girl said. "Well, I'm Margaret . . . but I suppose you know that. You have a strange accent. It's not Highland—I don't know what it is."

I ignored that. "Do you want to tell us why you were crying?"

"Certainly not. Why should I?"

"Oh, well, you seem to be better now."

When I pretended indifference she suddenly said: "Princess Mary was here."

"We saw her leaving."

"It's a grand honor for her to visit my father's house. Expensive, but an honor. Out of consideration for our situation—we're not wealthy—she brought only a small court, a hundred or so. But we had to feed them and put them up. Madam, my mother, has been preparing for it this month past and has made our lives miserable with cleaning and cooking and sewing. Father is a great friend of the Princess. She is his patroness."

"Did she enjoy herself?" I asked politely.

"If she did, I didn't!"

"Why not?"

"As a favor to my father, she has arranged a marriage for me—to a Spaniard of a noble family. Not the first son of course, because, after all, we're nobodies, but to a third son. It will set our family up a notch by connecting us to Spanish nobility."

"But you're much too young, aren't you?"

"I'm almost fifteen! I travel to meet him at the end of the year. We're assured he's very healthy with only a slight squint."

"Then why are you crying?"

"I'll have to live in Spain!" she wailed. "I'll have to leave my horse behind and my favorite wolfhound! —and I dearly love this house! I'm homesick already and I haven't even left yet!" A few more tears gathered and she choked them back and said crossly, "And there's so much to do to get ready!" She wiped her eyes and sniffed.

I thought, Why she's only three years older than I am and she's engaged! "Like bridal clothes?" I asked.

She nodded. "And linens. . . . Three dozen sheets and bolster cases with our initials entwined with true lovers' knots."

"Three dozen!" I gasped and looked at Heather. I didn't think our linen closet at home would even hold three dozen sheets!

Margaret said apologetically: "Oh, I know it's less than the usual number a bride brings to her new home, but they have made allowances. The Princess has arranged everything with them, and my family is very grateful about the reduced quantity—but I have to embroider them all!"

She was interrupted by a strange and terrible howl. We jumped. My heart seemed to miss a beat. The howl lingered on, its echo sounding like someone in pain. It seemed to be in the very walls. Heather grabbed my arm and hung on. We both stared around us, trying to discover where the terrible cry came from. Sometimes it was under our feet, sometimes in the ceiling. It chilled my blood and my scalp tingled. Heather's fingers dug into my arm. I tried to free it so I could put it around her, but she wouldn't loosen her grip. I stared at Margaret. "What was that?" I whispered.

Margaret forgot her tears and said easily, "Oh, don't be frightened. It's just our ghost, Old Tom." We stared at her. "Haven't you ever heard a ghost before?" Margaret asked, amused.

"No!" I said. But her look calmed me and I felt a little ashamed. Even Heather relaxed her hold and looked to her for more information. Also, the terrible echoes of the mournful cry were now dying away.

"Old Tom goes with the house. He was here when we took it over. We're quite used to him. My father says the castle in Northumberland where he was brought up had a poor female ghost who walked the upper hall. He says if you didn't step aside, she'd walk right through you and when she did your hair and beard crackled and your funnybone tingled."

I looked to see if she was joking. She wasn't. I said, "I'm not sure I believe in ghosts."

"Oh? You would if you lived in this old house," she said easily. "Now, what were we talking about?"

"Your marriage."

"Oh yes. . . ."

"You're still young. You should have some fun first."

She looked puzzled. "Fun? Is that the same as sport? . . . or pleasure? What do you mean?"

"It means you should give yourself time to enjoy life before you tie yourself down. You know, study, travel, see the world. Do something for yourself. That's what mother always tells us. It's your life. What do you want to do with it?"

But Margaret exploded. "Study? But that's all I've ever done! The one good thing about this marriage is I can get away from study! Why, I've learned French, German, Italian, Spanish and Greek—all in case I went to court someday as lady in waiting to Princess Mary. They thought perhaps I should have Portuguese too. . . . And naturally I read and write in Latin . . . and play the lute. Study! Don't mention study!"

"You speak all those languages?"

"Of course. My father hasn't stinted on tutors. He's out of the north and there they value education."

I said thoughtfully, "My brother is fifteen. He has a little French but no Latin."

"Is he dim-witted?"

"No!"

But Margaret looked unconvinced. "And you? What languages have you learned?" I thought wildly, what can I say?—a little French, a very little French. She was looking at me kindly. "Can you form your letters? If you're going to stay, I might teach you both to read. Are you serfs? I know we have some peasants in the family somewhere—up north, I think."

I told myself that she possibly didn't mean anything by it, but I said more sharply than I should, perhaps, "No, we're not!"

35

She looked at us both critically. "I see now you're quite clean-looking. I haven't seen gowns like that before. . . ."

"These are only our nightclothes."

"Oh, are you sleeping in the east wing? Madam, my mother didn't tell me anyone would be staying behind." I decided to let that go. She was looking at Heather, and Heather was looking back at her. "She hasn't spoken yet. Is she dumb? We have a child on the estate who is dumb."

"No, just shy."

"Oh, timorous. . . ."

Of course Heather isn't timorous at all! But like Don, she has a habit of watching and waiting in any strange situation. She has done it for weeks on end with new teachers at the beginning of term. I'm sure some of the nicer ones agonized over how they could break the news to our parents that she was not quite bright. The crisper ones simply summoned Mother to school and demanded to have Heather tested. Then they were in for a shock. She was doing it now with Margaret.

Then Heather's eyes left Margaret. She was taking in the room. She would, I know, be able to describe every last item when we compared notes later. She wandered over to the small arched fireplace and went to her knees on a white sheepskin rug in front of it because there was a wooden doll lying there in a red satin dress embroidered in gold and pearls with a wired, jeweled headdress. Heather held it up silently for me to admire. Margaret took note of our interest.

"The Princess brought me that poppet years ago on my birthing day. Her woodsman carved it and her ladies of the chamber dressed it. She always gifts us when she comes. I make pomander balls and lavendar wands for her."

I like visitors who bring gifts, myself. "What did she bring you this time?" I asked.

"Some comfits—and of course, the marriage proposal. Would you like a comfit?" She tried to jump up but stumbled on her heavy padded dress. She certainly couldn't move as easily as we could; she had wiring and boning and thick beaded embroidery on her bodice and couldn't bend in the middle at all easily. She couldn't turn her head too far, either, without jabbing her chin on her wired lace collar, which stood up all around. She had to push herself up, which looked very clumsy. "Let's eat something!" she cried. "Let's see what my page put in the livery cupboard for me."

She found a stool. She needed it to reach a cupboard with open-work carving that was hung high on the wall, and she brought out bread and wine and cheese.

"It's very inconvenient, isn't it? Why is it so high up?" I asked.

"Mice, you goose! Is it too cold in the North for mice to live?" She laughed and handed down to me small cakes and a pretty little wooden box decorated with paper frills. In it were the comfits.

She thought it odd when we refused the wine, but the bread was good and the cheese excellent, also the little cakes that were studded with almonds. The comfits were made of marzipan, brightly colored and made in fanciful shapes. Some had sugared violets on top and flecks of gold. I love marzipan, but Heather doesn't. She had taken one before she knew what it was and then didn't know how to get rid of it. While I diverted Margaret's attention, she slipped it into the pocket of her robe and took a little cake instead.

The three of us sat on the soft sheepskin happily eating. The glowing fire touched the white fleece with gold. Margaret had sandy hair and now it was turned to gold too. She sipped her wine from a pretty glass. It was much prettier than Father's wine glasses at home. I ate a second comfit. I knew I'd have to restrain myself and not pig it, for I dearly loved marzipan.

"Where do you come from?" Margaret asked as she popped a sugared almond into her mouth.

I glanced at Heather. She was rocking the doll absently as she munched a cake. I thought about it and said, "The Far West." This was no lie. Canada was certainly several thousand miles far west of Margaret's English home—and we were on the west coast of Canada. But as it hadn't yet been discovered, I thought I'd better not complicate things by saying anything more.

Margaret accepted this, but I soon realized that she was translating it to something quite different. She said: "My father came from the far west—from the Islands, the land of the Scots,—actually, the home of the MacDonalds. They say it's a wild place, rocky and bleak on the mainland and the Isles wildest of all. Do you come from the Isles?"

"Yes," I said and I crossed my fingers in the pocket of my robe.

"What is the name of your island?"

"Vancouver Island," I said boldly.

"There are many islands and I've only heard of them from friends of my father who have ventured into the northern wilds. The people are barbaric. They say they wear long shirts which they tie between their legs when they fight. They do say they are barefooted and bare-legged even in that north climate and that when it is too icy, they wrap themselves up in yards and yards of wool. They speak a strange tongue, too. Your speech is strange but I can understand you if you don't talk too fast."

Heather looked at me past the doll and her face had no more expression on it than what was painted on the wooden head in her arms. But I knew what she was thinking.

Margaret took another cake. "Perhaps Princess Mary left you behind to learn from us," she said. "Perhaps, if you have come from beyond the northern wall, she wants us to teach you civil ways. Madam, my mother hasn't told me yet. She is exhausted after the visit. No doubt, she'll call me to her chamber tomorrow and inform me." She sighed. "Putting on a party for royalty is a wearisome task—there are so many splendid dishes to make. We had a cockatrice."

"What's that?" I asked.

"I don't suppose you have anything so splendid in your wild islands, so I'll tell you. Our cook assembles it from parts of a rabbit and a cockerell—the front of one stuffed into the rear of the other—sewn together and arranged in a crouching position and cooked. When it's done, she glazes it to a dark, shiny brown and attaches a wooden head and decorates that. She gilds the cock's comb and the wattles and the beak and the claws at the front of the creature, and the rabbit claws at the rear. She attaches the wings with golden skewers—perhaps two sets of wings to make it more fanciful—and puts on a splendid tail, usually a pheasant's. When it's paraded in to the table on a bed of cress it's very exciting. The trumpets sound and we all clap and sing. Oh, our cook does make a splendid cockatrice!—but weren't you at the table to see it?"

"No, we missed it. Do you eat it?"

"Of course! What strange questions you do ask!"

"How do you cook a cockatrice?"

"The usual way, I suppose. You should ask my lady mother."

"What temperature? Three hundred fifty degrees or slower?" (My mother says temperature is very important and to always ask.)

"What very strange questions! Temperature! Things must be very different in the Isles."

"They are." Then I said something I knew that I shouldn't. But some imp seemed to take hold of my tongue. "We cook by electricity. Have you ever heard of electricity?"

"No. What is that?"

Heather was staring at me but I couldn't stop myself. "Have you ever stroked a black cat until its fur crackles and sparks? That's electricity."

"And you cook by that in the Isles?" Margaret's eyes were big.

"Yes."

"How do you hold the cat?"

I pretended I didn't hear. "What else did you have at the banquet?"

We could see her pulling her thoughts back from the cat. "Oh, she said, "the usual stargazey pies and hedgehogs." She reached for another sugared almond. "Guinea fowl, of course, sturgeon, pigeon pies, cold brawns —rennet shapes, quince jelly. . . . We had ten

40

courses. We had trenchers laid for one hundred and twenty. One hundred of the Princess's court and twenty of our own household." She looked at me. "What do you serve at a banquet in the Isles?"

I wished then I could describe something equally splendid but I could only bring to mind Baked Alaska or Cherries Jubilee. I didn't want to have to explain ice cream, so I settled on the Cherries Jubilee, which the grown-ups have but which we don't usually get a taste of. "We pour flaming brandy over cooked cherries," I said. "If the lights in the room are turned low, it's very pretty to see the blue flames curling around the dish."

"I shall inquire into that," Margaret said. "My Spanish in-laws will expect me to bring some new ideas from England. With the help of Madam, my mother, I am putting together a book of receipts. I suppose you have that very common pie, where larks fly out when it's opened?"

I thought again. "I haven't seen that myself, but sometimes at gentlemens' parties, there is a very large cake wheeled in and a girl jumps out."

Margaret threw back her head and clapped her hands. "A real girl? It would have to be a giant cake indeed to take all her great bundle of clothes! Dresses are bulky this year."

"No clothes." She looked so startled that I said quickly "More like a wood nymph in filmy draperies."

"Oh!" she cried, "How very droll!"

Actually, we never had such things at home. I had only seen this on old movies on television. Usually it was a party with all the men chomping on fat cigars. But someone in the family usually came along about then and turned the TV off. Anyway, I didn't mention the cigars because tobacco had not yet been brought back from Virginia. Was Walter Raleigh even born yet? Wasn't he the one who brought back from the New World both tobacco and potatoes? I wished I'd been keener about history. Nothing my teacher had ever said had prepared me for this! *"In 1492 Columbus sailed the ocean blue.* Hang on to that as a signpost," I told myself. But what year was this we were in now? Something in the 1550s. All this talk of Princess Mary—that was the clue. If I was at home, I'd look her dates up in my father's library. . . .

"I'll make a note of a Wood Nymph Pie in my journal," Margaret said. "Surely that will intrigue the Spanish! Now if there's anything you are curious about here, just ask and I'll try to explain it to you." She laughed. "It's going to be such a change for me to be teaching someone else! I'm so weary of being the pupil."

Before I could come up with anything suitable— for there were many things I wanted to ask about— Heather chose that moment to speak for the first time.

"I have a question," she said bouncing the doll on her knees. "Who is the man in your dungeon?"

CHAPTER FOUR

I caught my breath. I could have smacked her! Didn't Heather realize how this question would complicate things! Margaret stared at her in astonishment, first, that Heather really could talk, and then at the question. She said slowly, "I suppose the Princess must have told you." I was about to say, "Not the Princess," and stopped myself in time, for if the Princess had *not*, who could we say *had* told us? "Well, Father will be surprised!" Margaret breathed softly.

"How long has the prisoner been there?" Heather persisted.

"A long time, I think," Margaret almost whispered.

"Have you ever seen him?"

"Oh no. One of the stillroom maids told me she had heard there was a dungeon, but I don't know that there is really, or where it would be. The maids do prattle so."

"We know where it is," Heather announced flatly.

I didn't know how to shut her up! But secrets were of prime interest to my sister, and she was onto a good one now. I frowned and hoped she would look my way and get the message, but she was making sure our eyes didn't meet.

She said, "You get to it through the kitchen and down and then through the wine cellar. It's just beyond."

Margaret's eyes were big. "I've never been in the wine cellar. I've seldom been in the kitchen, if it comes to that."

"But tell us about the prisoner. We know he's there but we don't know why," Heather persisted.

"And I know why, I just don't know if he's still there or, in truth, if he ever was." Margaret thought about it for a moment, a troubled look upon her face. "I don't know if I should tell you the story or not—but if I don't you might do mischief."

"Quite right," I said and glared at my sister.

Heather, looking smug and still avoiding my eyes, was content now and sat smoothing the doll's hair—it was real hair and erupted in little tufts from numerous holes bored in its wooden scalp. She adjusted the jeweled headdress to her liking and waited.

Margaret began to speak. "My father was captured as a baby—his father and mother were killed by a warring clan foraging into the Highlands. He was found in his dead mother's arms and the soldier took him south to the castle in Northumberland. He was brought up there and taught civil ways. When he was of age, he became a mercenary, fighting for whomsoever paid him. Well, one day when he was out riding, this was in the south of England, he rescued a young girl who was being set upon by vagabonds. He chased them off and put her on her feet and rounded up her scattered attendants and found that he had rescued King Henry's daughter, Mary Tudor."

"Wow!" I said, thrilled.

"But she was in disfavor. Her father, the king, was

trying for a change of wife. To acknowledge the new one, he had to disown the old. He had to fight the church, which disapproved, fight his first wife, who refused to acknowledge she was not truly married to him, and fight their daughter, Mary, whom he now disowned. He banished the queen to one distant estate and his daughter Mary to another. Naturally, everyone was frightened of Henry and afraid to be civil to his daughter in case it provoked his displeasure. She was an abandoned, lonely young girl. And so those vagabonds set on her like the curs they were, and our soldier father, knowing nothing of the circumstances and doing it out of pure chivalry, scattered them with the flat of his sword across their backsides.

"Well, Princess Mary was eternally grateful to Donald MacDonald, our father. When times got better for her, she sought him out and honored him. She gave him these acres, which had been hers from her mother, Catherine of Aragon, and the manor on it. My father brought his young family to it."

"My brother's name is Donald MacDonald," I said. At that moment I felt lonely for him and wished he was there.

"They nearly all are," Margaret answered. "I, too, have a brother, Donald."

"What about the dungeon?" Heather prompted.

"Yes. . . . So everything went well for the Princess until a strange man, a seer, a mystic, began wandering the streets, crying out that Mary Tudor would be queen of England some day, but that she would be known as Mary the Bloody. He said she would be childless and that a trollop's daughter would succeed to the throne. He said Mary would die unhappy. . . .

45

"Mary was upset. She had a half-brother who was on the throne now; she didn't even wish to be queen. But she didn't like being called Bloody and having nasty things said about her. Her half-sister, the small Princess Elizabeth, was, in Mary's opinion and her Queen mother's, certainly the daughter of a trollop. She couldn't argue that!—but she tried to overlook it and was kind to the clever child, for it was no fault of Elizabeth's who her mother was."

"Go on. . . ." said Heather as Margaret stopped for breath.

"By chance on a market day, Father heard the seer spewing out his poison to the crowd. He ordered him to cease his rantings about the Princess. The man refused. Father told us he kicked him in the backside all around the village common. The fellow hopped ahead of him and yelped and the crowd laughed but he still wouldn't hold his wisht. So Father had the blackguard picked up and brought here. The scurvy tramp was frightened, of course. He shouted that if he died, he'd leave a curse on this family. But Father was strong of purpose. He said that in that case, he must make sure nothing happened to him. He clapped him in the dungeon for safety's sake and promised to take excellent care of him. The seer screamed that when he did die, '. . . the father and the first-born son of every second generation of the Mac-Donalds of Austwick Manor would die in some unseemly way,' and he cursed Father vilely. But Father has made sure the knave stayed alive. He feeds him well, sends the apothecary when needed, gives him blankets and a fire. The Princess was grateful that Father stifled the fool. She says she's eternally in our father's debt. That's why she's so kind to me and my brothers and sisters and has found me a husband—only I wish, oh, how I wish I didn't have to leave home!" She sighed and went on. "Perhaps she'll find a place at court for my brother Donald and the twins."

"But how terrible for the seer!" I said. "To be kept in a dungeon ever after! Isn't that cruel?"

Margaret looked surprised. "Why no! My father's a great fighter and could have killed him on the spot! He stands for no nonsense, does my father."

"And there was the curse," Heather pointed out. "He couldn't kill him because of that, could he?"

Margaret startled us then by suddenly laughing and clapping her hands. "Oh, we don't believe in the curse! In all the years nothing the wretch has said has come to pass!"

"But do you think the story is true?" I asked.

"Perhaps it's just something my father tells around the fire to amuse us when the gales are blowing out of the north. He's a powerful, amusing man, is my father," and she smiled around at us proudly.

"You'd better believe it, Margaret, because—"

"Heather!" I snapped. "Have another cake!"

But I was worried. While I didn't know if the story was exactly true, I knew, and Heather did, that there was certainly a wretched but well-fed figure in the dungeon, with blankets and a brazier for warmth, just as the story told. If that was true, was the curse true? It struck me now as it hadn't before, that our very own father had died from an unexpected accident—fishing from a sturdy boat on a calm sea in Oak Bay. No one could ever explain it, Mother said. So was ours the "every other generation" of the curse? Surely it was important to find that out—because the question then was:

How about our brother, Don—was he in danger? He was the firstborn son of this generation who inherited. Was he, like our father, doomed? I stared unblinking into the blaze of the logs and worried the idea like a dog with a bone.

Margaret suddenly yawned. She recovered quickly and said, "I beg your pardon. . . . but indeed it's been a very long day. We hawked and hunted hard all morning in the forest with the Princess's court—then had to dress for the banquet and had mummers afterward. I cannot contain my yawning any longer."

I took the hint. "It's very late. We must go."

Margaret scrambled to her feet and smoothed down the nap of her blue velvet dress. Heather laid aside the doll reluctantly and we left the warm circle of the fire and walked to the door.

"Can you find your way back to your room?" she asked politely.

"Yes," I answered. "Good night, Margaret."

She stepped out into the chilly hall with us and gave us candles from a side table. "Tomorrow I'll hear from Madam, my mother what the Princess desires done for you. Lessons for sure and grooming, I think. Well, good night, Hillary. Good night, Heather." She gave us a smile and a little wave and went back to her room and closed her door.

We were unused to carrying candles. I soon found that if I tipped mine even a little it dripped grease, and if I moved too fast, it sputtered and threatened to leave me to the freezing dark. I learned quickly how to protect the flame with my cupped hand as we moved down the creaking stairs.

The two small moving points of our candles didn't

reach the portraits on the walls high above us, but did flicker dimly on the steel suit of armor at the bend of the staircase. Here, the great window showed only a patch of slatey gray that did nothing to help us on our way. And it was bitterly cold. We met no one in the hall— everyone would be sitting over a late fire or would be already huddled in his goose-feather bed. Anyway, no one left the circle of his hardly won warmth to investigate our passing, and we moved as silently as ghosts down the stairs and through the lower hall.

CHAPTER FIVE

WE SLEPT IN LATE. MOTHER CAME INTO OUR ROOM and ran up the blinds. "Well, I know it's Sunday, but you've never slept in this long before. Remember, we have one more crate to open. Wakee! Wakee!" She bustled out again.

I sat up and Heather blinked over the edge of her blanket. She looked around dazed. She whispered, "I dreamed of the house, Hil!"

"So did I. We were talking to. . . ."

". . . to Margaret."

"Sitting on a sheepskin rug."

"Yes, and there was a doll dressed in red with a jeweled cap. It didn't seem like a dream."

"I don't think it was," I said.

We sat on the edge of our beds, each of us staring at our toes thoughtfully, as if we hadn't seen them before.

"You remember about the seer in the dungeon? If that story was true, what about Don? And our very own father is already dead."

"By unforeseen accident." We were silent, thinking about it.

"Are we going to tell the family?" she asked.

"We have to!"

"How are we going to make them believe?"

I thought it was no good stampeding with fright for Don. "But we don't know for sure yet. This might not be the 'every second generation.' Accidents like what happened to our father could happen at any time, so it doesn't follow that this has to be the one. No, this might not be the generation to look out for at all."

Heather looked stubborn. "But we have to make sure, Hil, and warn him."

"But could a warning prevent it—if it were fated to be?"

"Perhaps some extra-good person could remove the curse."

"That's just in stories, Heather!"

"Well, you suggest something," she said raising her voice.

But I couldn't think of a thing to suggest, so we went down to breakfast.

Mother brought a pile of toast to the table. "Let's get breakfast over with, then we can open the picture crate. We left it until you were here, Don," she said.

We sat down in front of our porridge. Heather always puts honey on hers, I use brown suger. I guess we didn't feel like talking much. I know I was as tired as if I hadn't slept at all; besides, I wouldn't have known where to start to tell them. I wanted to think about it for a while.

"Cat got your tongue?" Don said looking at us.

For answer we shoved the strawberry jam over. He took it and promptly forgot about us. But Mother was looking our way.

"You girls were up last night. I found milk glasses on the dining table this morning."

"We couldn't sleep," I said.

"Too much excitement yesterday. It was rather like Christmas, wasn't it?"

"We . . . we kind of dreamed of the house."

"So did I," said Mother cheerfully.

We glanced at her over our spoons. I said carefully, "What did you dream?"

"Oh, just that we seemed to be pulling nails forever—you know, general packing-case mess to clean away."

"And what did you girls dream of?" Father asked.

I said, "We didn't dream exactly. We met Margaret MacDonald."

"And who is that?"

"The girl in the small chamber."

"So you've given them names already," he said.

"No. That's her name," said Heather looking him in the eye.

"How do you know?"

"She told us."

"And you were both in the same dream?"

"Yes—only we don't think it was a dream."

"Now that's very interesting and peculiar," said Father. "Are you sure?"

"Yes."

"A likely story," said Don and laughed.

"Oh, I don't know," said Father. "Your mother and I have the same dreams." He looked at her and they both smiled, but I don't think they were talking about the same kind of dream.

After breakfast we opened the picture crate. Father

and Don did it between them and they drew out an oil painting in an ancient gold frame and we all stood back and looked at it.

It was a very dark painting, but a man's hawklike face floated up from a murky background that might have been the oak paneling of a room. He held a leather-bound book in his long fingers and his elbow rested easily on a table covered with a Persian rug. The splendid brocaded sleeves of his tunic bulged through a sleeveless robe that was a dark black-red. This was pleated like a choir robe. He had a heavy gold chain that disappeared behind the book and a sheathed sword lay on the table beside him. But it was his face that was striking. We looked from it to Don in surprise. He had the same red beard as the doll, but there was the high-bridged nose, the same deep-set blue eyes and, of course, the long hands folded around the book. In the top corner in Roman block letters was his name and the date: Anno Domini 1556.

Father stared at Don as we were all doing and said, "Mr. Willoughby was right! There's no doubt who you are!"

Don was uncomfortable with all eyes turned on him. But I think he was rather pleased—more pleased with the portrait than he had been with the model of the house, which he was afraid would be labeled a "doll's house."

Mother laughed ruefully. "He's my son, too. Wouldn't you think there would be something of my side of the family in him."

Don said gruffly, "The girls look like him. I'm not the only one with the look."

He was right. Heather had it and so did I, but we

had escaped the nose, thank goodness. Still we examined each other critically and looked at our long hands and measured the length of our fingers while they hung the picture above the fireplace in the place of honor.

Heather said, "I wish we had met him when we met Margaret."

I nodded. "We could have. He was only across the hall."

"What was that, dear?" asked Mother setting aside the Picasso print they had just taken down to make room for the ancestor.

"I said, I wish we had met him last night. We could have."

"In your dream, you mean?"

"It wasn't a dream. We only saw Margaret. She was tired though. They'd just had a great feast for Princess Mary. She had just left with all her people, and Margaret said the family was bushed."

I saw Mother glance at Father. Don gave Heather a cheerful little shove and said, "You're nuts, you know that?" and she turned fast and shoved him back.

"We did too talk to her! She's only fifteen and she knows French and German and Italian and Greek and Latin! She's not a dope like you! She even asked us if you were dim-witted."

Don let out a hoot and Mother moved fast to separate them.

"What's going on here!?" he demanded. "I have to defend myself against a rotting rag doll called Margaret? Is everybody crazy?" He waved his arms at us helplessly and started to storm out.

"Wait," said Father, and he wasn't smiling now. "If you're going to the gym, take your bike. I'd rather you didn't come back with that Charlie. You might have recovered from the crack-up in his car, but your mother and I have not."

The family always argued over Charlie. It wasn't that Don doted on Charlie—he didn't—as much as Charlie hung around Don. It was our opinion that Charlie was attracted to our brother because he was so good at sports—at anything he attempted—like being the lead in the school play, or the editor of the annual. Don was a school personality and there were lots of kids who liked to be seen in his company. But Charlie was over seventeen and he had a good car all to himself. That was the kind of family he had! They supplied him with a sports car and I heard that he liked to drawl in a bored voice that it had ". . . twenty coats of candy-apple red lacquer on it, a special job." Don wasn't exactly envious, he was much too busy, but he always accepted a ride when offered, and it seemed Charlie was always waiting after games or rehearsals or editorial meetings and offering. And it was true that there had been a nasty accident with Charlie coming out of it scot free, but Don pretty badly banged up. Anyhow, Don knew better than to bring Charlie to the house—which was strange, because our parents were usually happy to welcome all our friends. And so the rest of us hadn't met Charlie. The candy-apple red sports car (now repaired and with still more coats of new lacquer) would roar up in front of our house and stop on a dime, and Don would hop out of it and come in without a backward glance, and the car would streak away leaving rubber on the fast turn at the corner. I had often glimpsed the car hanging around the high school. It was wild. I wish I could have ridden in it. But Charlie didn't know I was alive.

Now Don complained to Father. "You make it tough. He hangs around and waits for me. I can't be rude."

"You have our permission," said Father.

We heard the front door slam as Don went off unhappily and thundered down the front steps.

Mother said quietly, "Perhaps Don feels that if he begged off now, Charlie would think him afraid to drive with him again. Don wouldn't like that. But I agree, I wish he wouldn't."

"It might be embarrassing to him, I quite see that, but it has to be stopped. I don't like anything I hear about this Charlie."

There was a long and uncomfortable silence before our parents turned back to the picture. Mother said one more thing though. She said, "I don't know why you enjoy annoying your brother so, Heather."

"He never believes anything we say," she grumped.

"Well, if you must say things like that."

Heather was an arguer. I punched her to pipe down, but she shook me away and said, "Margaret thought *I* was dumb. Hil put her right about that. *I* didn't get mad at Margaret. Why does he have to get mad?"

Mother looked at her silently, then she said, "I think we've had too much excitement altogether. Let's try to get back to normal, shall we?" and she steered both of us to the kitchen. "Let's get some dishes done around here, eh?"

I thought doing dishes was a little too normal. I said, "Margaret doesn't do dishes. Margaret has hardly ever been in the kitchen." Mother said nothing. I thought it might be better to have lived in the old Tudor house . . . but then I thought of marrying a

Spanish noble with a squint, instead of seeing the world first and doing something interesting, and I wasn't so sure I'd like to be ordered to do that. Better to do dishes, for the moment.

Several times I got Mother alone and tried to tell her about the seer and the curse and the "every second generation," but she just laughed. I walked to the public library—one mile—with Father so that I could get him alone and tell him Margaret's story. He was interested and listened very carefully and when I'd finished said he thought I had the makings of a writer and told me all the courses to take at college that would be helpful. I was getting nowhere! It didn't seem fair to talk to Don about it—even if he would listen.

Heather too was giving them the story and talking about the beautiful doll and just how it was dressed. They listened and were amused at first. Mother kept saying, "But of course it was just a dream. You're weaving a story around the house dolls."

And we said "No! No! We're not! Honestly, we're not!"

But our nagging did some good. One day as we talked of Margaret and the house, Mother suddenly said, "All right, show me! Let's settle this once and for all."

We were delighted and excited. I was more than eager to prove it. "We'll try tonight! Wear something warm! These English houses are awfully cold."

"That's a date," said Mother gaily. "I'll wear my fur coat." Father looked up from the paper he was reading and smiled.

She did, too. When our alarm woke us up and we went out to the dining room, there was Mother, cookies and milk ready on the table and her fur coat around her shoulders, and Father ready to wave us off. "I put out the cookies in case eating is part of the magic," she said.

"Oh I don't think so. It was just why we happened to be out here," I said.

"Well, what do we do now?"

"We just walk towards it slowly. You'll see a gravel drive, and a bridge over a moat with ducks and swans."

"If we don't eat the cookies, we can feed them to the ducks," said Mother lightly. And I had a feeling of misgiving, as if she wasn't taking it seriously enough.

"We'll eat them," said Heather.

I took one of Mother's hands and Heather took the other and we led her across the carpet. The Tudor house looked shadowed but peaceful under the faint glow coming into the dining room from outside. *This is the way to prove it*, I thought. *Now she'll have to believe us!*

We stepped off the carpet. No gravel squeaked under our slippers, no lights showed in Margaret's windows, no bridge, no moat, no swans. We advanced until our chins were almost touching the eaves and had to stop.

"It isn't working," whispered Heather. "Why isn't it working?"

"Wait!" I begged and held them both there. But nothing, absolutely nothing, happened! I could have wept.

Mother led us back to the table. "Let's eat," she said. "Cookie? Milk?"

"Perhaps there's some pie left," said Father watching us with concern, I thought.

"It should have worked!" I cried. "It worked for us!"

"Well, it's a nice thought," Mother said. "But it's

just a fancy. It's a lovely house. I quite like it myself. The important thing, girls, is to know fact from fiction. Enjoy the fancy, but keep it in its place." She patted my hand. "We all think you could grow up to be a writer, Hillary. You could if you'd tend to your spelling more. You too, Heather, dear. You could be like the Brontë sisters and entertain each other with stories. I think that's just what you're doing now, isn't it?"

I couldn't speak. I was afraid if I tried, I'd break into tears. I bit my lip hard and couldn't swallow the cookie. Mother patted my hand again. "Don't, dear. I quite understand."

"She's frustrated," said Heather. "And so am I."

"Come to bed now, both of you."

They herded us upstairs ahead of them, kissed us both and tucked us in and left us. I thought Mother's step was lighter as she went down the hall with Father.

I tried to talk about it to them the next day, but Mother said, "When a joke is kept up too long it becomes a bore." When she spoke like that we knew she meant it. We didn't exactly sulk but we were stubbornly silent at meals.

Then one day shortly after, Mother went into our room to round up the laundry. She went along our hangers looking for school blouses and came to our dressing gowns. She backed out of the closet holding them up. "Your best robes!" she called. "What are these spots? It looks like grease."

We gathered around to examine them. We looked from the spots to her. "It must be candle grease," I said. "Margaret gave us candles to light our way downstairs. The hall was drafty and blew the flame around." The hall was drafty and blew the flame around."

Mother looked exasperated. "You've been playing

with matches. I don't like that. Do you want to set the house on fire?"

I said, "Mother, I'm twelve years old! I'm very careful with matches. But we didn't need matches. Margaret just lit them from one already burning on the upper landing."

Mother stared at us and then went out to find Father. We waited uncomfortably. We hadn't meant to mention Margaret again—and now this.

She returned with Father and he sat down on the edge of a bed and looked at us solemnly. We knew we were in for a lecture. Meanwhile, Mother stood to one side clutching the robes.

"Now girls," Father began, "we've got to put an end to this game. It really is . . . is . . . is. . . ."

While he was feeling for words and we were standing at attention ready to say, "Yes sir. . . . No sir. . . ." Mother let out a little yelp. We all looked around. She had her hand in the pocket of Heather's robe, and she brought out a slightly squashed comfit and held it up. "What's this?" she cried.

We didn't say anything. Father poked it curiosuly. "It looks like a little cake—a petit-four."

"I've never seen such a fancy one," said mother. "It didn't come from our local bakery."

Father turned to us. "Who gave it to you?"

"You won't get mad?" I asked.

"Of course not."

"Princess Mary brought them to Margaret and Margaret had them in her livery cupboard. She shared with us. They're marzipan—Heather doesn't like marzipan. She stashed it in her pocket so as not to offend Margaret."

A long silence followed this. Mother looked upset but Father said to Mother gently, "Sh . . . Mary " and turned back to us. "Now let's look at this beautiful little cake."

"Comfit," said Heather in a small voice. "They're comfits and they came in a wooden box with a paper frill around the edge."

"Comfit," said Father dutifully. "What's this on top?"

Mother peered at it. "A sugared violet," she said.

Father poked at it. "And gold flakes. . . . What bakery uses gold flakes?"

"It can't be real, George."

"It certainly looks it." He turned to us. "Well, we'll say no more about it for now, but you do see how all this upsets your mother. And you know this is no time to upset her with the new baby coming. You understand that, don't you?"

We murmured we were sorry, and he led Mother from the room with his arm around her. She was still clutching our robes and the squashed comfit.

Nothing more was said for a couple of days, then he came and told us he had had the flake of gold tested and it was real gold leaf and would we like to tell him anything more about it. So we eagerly told him everything again, and we leaned on the story of the vagabond seer and the curse. And we managed to make him see that if Mother was worried about us, we were more worried about Don.

He listened and was soothing, but I don't know how much he believed. He still wanted to talk about "our imaginations," but then he'd come back to the candle grease and the squashed comfit in Heather's pocket and he'd fall strangely silent. Also, I think he had been making a search of all the fancy French bakeries in town trying to trace it and asking around among our friends if they had someone in Europe who sent them presents like this. But no one had. He looked very puzzled.

Time went on and just when we thought we were getting the truth across to them, something would be said that showed we weren't at all. They seemed to forget any proof so quickly. Especially Mother. One evening at the table, she put on that extra bright, enthusiastic look that I knew was supposed to take our minds off things. "Next month is your birthday, Heather," she announced. "Have you thought about the kind of party you'd like? Mullins is making up a beautiful ice cream cake these days. Would you like me to order one?"

Heather thought about it. She thought and thought until I could see Mother's interest was wearing thin but she said cheerily, "Well, there's lots of time."

As she was turning away, Heather spoke. "I've thought. No ice cream cake, thank you. I'd rather have a feast."

Don grinned. "A feast? What do you have at a feast?"

Heather didn't hesitate. She said, "A stargazey pie, cold brawn, rennet shapes, a hedgehog, quince jelly and a cockatrice."

Father laughed and reached for his coffee. "What, no boar's head?"

Heather said solemnly. "I've never seen a boar's head in our butcher's case. But a cockatrice is possible, I think. I can tell him how to prepare it. Margaret explained it to us."

They stared at her and I watched to see how they

would take this. Well, Don was looking at her as if she was crazy, Mother was plainly disturbed again, but Father remained calm. "That's quite a menu. How did you come to think it up?"

"Margaret told us that's what they had when they entertained Mary Tudor—and a lot more. Right, Hil?"

"Right," I said. "Things like sturgeon and pigeon pie. I told her about Cherries Jubilee. I only hope I got it right, Mother."

As no one said anything Heather took it that it was settled and said, "May we leave the table now, please?"

"Yes, dear," said Mother absently.

We were no sooner around the corner and into the hall when we heard Father say, "Stop worrying, Mary! You have a ten-foot shelf of cookbooks. They've lived with discussions of chestnut stuffings and sauces for years. What do you expect?"

"Practical cookbooks!" cried Mother. "I didn't know half of what they were talking about! They didn't hear about a stargazey pie or a hedgehog in this kitchen!"

Don said, "How to cook a hedgehog might be in one of those survival cookbooks. You know, 'How to Live Off the Land if the Worst Happens'."

"First catch a hedgehog." Father laughed and he went off to the bookshelves and began to look at mother's cookbooks, to see what we'd been reading, I suppose.

Meanwhile Mother was at our biggest dictionary flipping through the C's, muttering "cockatrice, cockatrice. . . ."

Don, unconcerned as usual, wandered off to the front room where we saw him stand for a moment looking at his ancestor and feeling his own nose. Then he took off for the gym.

"You've given them something to think about," I said to Heather.

"But it never seems to do any good!" she wailed.

She was right. It didn't.

CHAPTER SIX

ONE MORNING SOON AFTER THIS, MISS MARTIN, THE visiting school psychologist sent for me. We were in the middle of a spelling test when the order came for me to report to her office, and I knew it had to be important to pull me out of class. My teacher grumped but let me go. I didn't mind missing the exam at all and went down the hall wondering what was up.

Miss Martin with her gray hair blued to the color of a hydrangea smiled widely as I came in. So I hadn't done anything! I sighed with relief and congratulated myself again on missing the test.

"I'm Hillary MacDonald. You sent for me, Miss Martin?"

"Oh Hillary, I just heard about your wonderful English dollhouse. I'd love to see it. Tell me all about it."

I looked at her in surprise and was immediately suspicious. As if she would send for me to talk about dollhouses in the middle of class! She must have thought I was born yesterday. "What dollhouse?" I asked, annoyed for Don's sake. He didn't want to be known as "the guy who owns a doll's house." He always made us

65

refer to it as "the model." So I looked her in the eye as if I didn't know what she was talking about.

Her smile stayed in place but her eyes flicked. "Now Hillary, it's no secret. Your mother mentioned it to me at the PTA the other day."

So mother was in on this, I thought. "Did she say 'dollhouse'?" I asked.

"Well, perhaps not. I just took it that it was." I remained silent. She looked annoyed. (Was I getting to be like Heather and Don in using silence? It had its uses.) After waiting for me to speak, she said brightly, "She says you're quite taken with it—that you've made an imaginary playmate out of a doll called Margaret." Her voice dropped playfully. "I had an imaginary playmate when I was little. I called her Nellie."

I said politely, "Did you? That must have been very interesting."

"Well, isn't it?"

"I've never had one," I answered. "I don't know."

"Don't you want to tell me about the doll you call Margaret?"

"If you mean the doll in the blue dress, it's a small rag doll about five inches high. Its face is embroidered on linen and it's very, very old."

"What do you think of it?"

"Think? Well, I wonder who made them all."

"What else? Do you talk to her? Does she talk to you?"

I stared at her, then said gently, "Miss Martin, this is a very old doll—there are no buttons to push to make her say ma-ma, even if we were allowed to handle her. I don't think you understand. Father says they're museum pieces."

She went on eagerly just as if I hadn't spoken. "Does she discuss food with you? My imaginary friend used to say things like, 'Let's go ask for some ice cream,' and we did, and I'd say to my mother, 'Nellie says she wants some ice cream, please.'" Miss Martin laughed and laughed and clapped her dimpled hands together at the memory.

"We're not much for talking to dolls at our house," I said.

Miss Martin stopped laughing and looked both disappointed and annoyed. "Well, dear, I was hoping you'd tell me all about it because I do really love dollhouses— it's almost a passion with me." She picked up some papers and started to read, dismissing me. She said a little grimly, "You'd better get back to class and perhaps we can talk about it again when we have more time."

I was just going into my room when the door on the other side of the hall opened and Heather came out. "Where are you going?" I whispered.

"Miss Martin sent for me."

"She's trying to pump us about Margaret! I didn't tell her a thing!"

My teacher saw me lingering and hissing at the door and ordered me in. Heather went off down the hall.

I had to make up the test after school. When I was free to find Heather, I said eagerly, "Well? What happened?"

Heather looked worried. "You know something? Miss Martin had a playmate called Nellie. Isn't that crazy? She told me all about her."

"What about Margaret?"

"Who?" asked Heather. "Oh, I just got her talking about Nellie. Nellie had black, snapping eyes and could

67

talk to turtles. I didn't know Miss Martin was such a weirdo, did you? Why turtles? Do you think the principal knows about it?"

It became clear to us that Mother was very worried about us and we were sorry about that because of her condition. One day we overheard her talking on the telephone to someone and the tone of her voice really made us feel low. She didn't hear us come in the back way because of our sneakers. She was saying urgently, "I know children frequently have invisible playmates! You don't need to explain that to me! But ours never have! They've had each other. They play together happily—always have!" There was a long silence while someone talked at the other end. "No, no!" she cried. "It isn't that! I know it isn't that! This girl Margaret they talk about is older. She talked about Elizabethan food and embroidering true lovers' knots and getting married in Spain. No, I tell you . . . ! Well, wouldn't you be worried?—because they're not really happy about it! They're depressed. I can't understand it. Yes, I *am* worried."

I nudged Heather and we backed out silently and sat on the back step until we heard Mother hang up and return to the kitchen, then we went in noisily and asked for milk. She turned a cheery face to us—just as if she hadn't been so worried a moment before—and found some custards and sat down at the other side of the table and had some herself. (She had to eat for two, she said.) I was surprised at how Mother could hide her feelings. I wanted to make it easier for her, but I wanted to save Don too, and I didn't know how to do it alone.

In a light voice that was falsely cheerful, Mother

asked, "How's Margaret?" This surprised us. I think she was forcing herself to accept our quirks—that's what she thought it was, a quirk.

"All right, I guess," I said carefully.

"You haven't seen her lately in your dreams?"

"We only met her once—and it wasn't a dream."

"You were overtired that night. No wonder you had bad dreams."

"It wasn't bad. More interesting than anything."

"We haven't tried to go back," said Heather.

"I should hope not!" said Mother.

I began to get nervous in case Mother made us promise that we wouldn't go back—or something like that. So I wished Heather would shut up—it was that kind of a moment.

But Mother didn't. Then I thought, of course, she wouldn't, because she didn't believe in it! Hadn't she offered to go with us and hadn't we failed to produce Margaret? That would settle it in her mind. She thought it was just a dream, and you can't make yourself dream the same thing again, so she would think it silly to ask us to promise. No, she was ignoring the things, the small proofs, we gave her, and she was determined to think it was just some romantic quirk that had taken our fancy, and she was annoyed that we wouldn't move on to something else—some new craze, like the return of the yoyo or the hula hoop, or pine for one of the latest electronic games that answered you back. Anyway the moment passed without us having to promise anything.

She repeated Heather's question. "Why? Because it seems to have upset you."

"Because you won't believe us," wailed Heather. "And because we're worried about Don! What if what

Margaret said about the soothsayer and his curse is true? What if this is another 'every second generation'? It's already happened to our father. It could happen to Don!"

Mother said suddenly that she felt like lying down and would we please try to be quiet and let her rest.

After she had gone up to her room, we sat on at the table. We couldn't think why the candle wax and the comfit didn't prove our story was true!

"If we could bring a comfit back, how about bringing back something bigger . . . ?" I said thoughtfully.

"Like the doll!" Heather cried. "Do you think Margaret would let us? She's past playing with dolls. She's getting married."

"Well, we could ask to borrow it. But if the Princess gave it to her I don't think she'd want to give it up."

"But we could ask."

We were worried now that it might not work. It hadn't the last time with Mother. Supposing it didn't ever again. We decided that we would test it that very night, and we ignored the idea that we might have seen Margaret for the last time. So we got our skates and went out so as to leave the house quiet for Mother, and Heather made up little songs about the red doll and skated furiously at the prospect of having it.

When we went in an hour or so later, Father was home. He and Mother had a surprise for us. "Notice anything different?" he asked cheerfully.

As they were standing beside the model looking pleased, we went and peered through the windows. They had changed the dolls! The Margaret doll had gone, also MacDonald, the father, at the writing desk, and the mother at the embroidery frame, and the cook in the kitchen—all had gone! We were allowed to spring open the front of the dungeon and we saw that the villainous seer was gone, too. Now, a woman doll in black silk with a tiny cap and veil was at the desk in the big chamber and different servants were in the kitchen. Father had gone into the deep drawer and taken out the next set of dolls and put the first set back!

Mother said: "We thought it would be interesting to change them . . . like a museum changes its exhibits."

We said it was very nice—but we knew why they had done it!

We decided that we would still try to go back. Heather had Margaret's doll firmly in mind and wasn't going to give up that easily. But we wished they hadn't put her away.

That night, we waited until everyone was asleep. Twice Heather drifted off and I had to awaken her. At last it was midnight. We climbed into our warm robes and crept down to the dining room. We took each other's hands and moved slowly toward the house in the bay window. But we were very nervous this time. . . . Then once again we felt the softness of the rug turn into the crunch of gravel. "It's working!" I breathed. Heather answered by tightening her fingers around mine. We saw that the manor was lit up—every last window—and that shadows moved in all the rooms; the household seemed very active. It was raining a fine but determined rain. In the driveway around the entrance, a few cloaked people stood talking together and disregarding it.

We approached slowly. "It looks different," whispered Heather.

Something certainly was different. Even the trees of the park seemed to be taller and darker—the shrubs at the steps were more dense and reached out to lay their wet leaves over the backs of the stone leopards as if to give them cover. We walked past the men ruffed like turkey-cocks and hunched against the wet, who only glanced at us idly and went on talking, and were about to put our hands to the knob of the great door when it was opened from within and someone pulled us through roughly.

A woman had jerked us in. She looked down at us sharply and snapped, "You're late! What's that you're wearing? Did you bring your black clouts?"

We saw that the entrance hall was crowded with people and that they were all wearing rusty black, some almost in rags; a few were sitting on the bottom step of the staircase as if waiting for something to happen. They were an unkempt lot.

I didn't know what she meant. It seemed right to say no, so I said it.

She hissed like a goose through gaps in her discolored teeth. "What do you think you're being paid for? You good-for-nothing little besoms!" and pushed me roughly ahead of her.

I shook off her hand, which was none too clean. "No one is paying us anything," I said and dug in my heels. "I am Hillary MacDonald and this is my sister, Heather."

The woman pulled back at once. "Oh, you're family. Well, they're in the great hall, beyond. You'll stand with them. But you'd better go upstairs and get something to cover you. I don't know who you're supposed to be in that get-up."

The people waiting around stared rudely and some grinned. They all had long white tapers not yet lit. We pushed through the squatters and picked our way up the stairs.

The door to Margaret's room stood open and a woman in a large white apron who might have been a ladies' maid was on the landing just outside it. She said, "Latecomers! I suppose they sent you up for a robe." There was a pile of black garments on a chair nearby and from it she handed me a mass of black poplin and found another for Heather. "Try these for length. Hook them close. You'll have to hide all that unseemly color— and where are your ruffs? You're only half-dressed. How could your maid turn you out so? She needs shaking up, that one! But you are no doubt one of the crowd come down from the North. What a calamity! First the dear master, then his heir! Lackaday! And all in a month's time!"

As I pulled the robe on and hooked it at the neck, I went to the door of Margaret's room and peeked in. It looked different. Now the desk was against a side wall and above it was a shelf to hold the books. There was no sheepskin rug, but a small oriental one before the fireplace. On the mantel was the model of a galleon in full sail, and above it, crossed swords. A game of chess had been set up on a table near the bed and abandoned, the pieces all toppled.

"Where are you from?" the woman asked.

"The islands," I said quickly and she accepted it as Margaret had.

"Where's Margaret?" demanded Heather.

"Which one do you mean? There's more than one Margaret in the house this sad day. . . . There, you'll do. You're likely the last that's needing black."

"This is Margaret's room," said Heather not budging.

"Oh, no, my pretty. This is . . . was . . . the young master's room!" She wiped her eyes with her apron. "See, there's the game just as he was playing with his tutor only last week. Lord save his lady mother in her double dose of grief!" She wiped her eyes again. "It's the villainous soothsayer's words come true, that's what it is! What to do! What to do!" She controlled herself and after a minute said more calmly, "I know of two Margarets here for the services. There might even be more from a distance that I know nought about and staying at the village inn. What was your Margaret like?"

"She was sandy-haired and fifteen, and she was family."

"I don't know who that can be. There's a wee Margaret, a bairn for sure, and t'other is an old lady aunt down from London town."

Heather looked stubborn and about to argue. I said quickly, "Who are all those people at the bottom of the stairs?"

"Why, the hired mourners of course. You don't think that scruffy lot is family, do you? Where've you been all your life, lass?"

A distant bell began to toll. The woman quickly undid her white apron and tossed it aside and now appeared in severe black. She herded us ahead of her briskly and we started down the stairs, our black poplin billowing around us. "And remember to sign the guest book," she whispered hoarsely. "And no unseemly running or skipping."

In the hall below, the mourners, their tapers now

lit, were forming into two lines facing the front door. The woman steered us through their ranks to a large book open on the candle table, where a quill pen and ink were laid out.

"Sign!" she whispered.

I looked at the pen curiously and signed. I had never dipped into ink before. Heather signed and made a bad blot. The woman tutted at her as she sprinkled sand on it out of a kind of pepper pot and said our handwriting was no credit to us or our governess. It certainly looked strange on that page of curlicue writing—plain and no nonsense of fancy tails to it. I could have added a flourish to mine, but she steered us through the wide doors into the room beyond and told us to find our parents and stay close to them. We said nothing to this but moved toward the great log fire to get warm and look about us.

There were many splendidly dressed people assembled: women all in black, full-skirted dresses, and men in black velvet doublets and hose. There were children also, dressed in imitation of the adults. The stiff white ruffs which everyone wore were the only accent in all that blackness, except for the red brocade at the windows and the richness of the tapestry on the wall.

A middle-aged woman with a stricken look took her position at the head of this company. The maid stepped up and placed a black veil over her head; it covered her face completely and cascaded over her shoulders down to her elbows. The other people fell into two lines behind her and hushed their children.

Another bell sounded and I heard the front door open. Cold night air stirred the hem of my robe and chilled my ankles. Suddenly the mourners in the outer hall lifted their heads and began to wail. A baby in a nurse's arms jumped and screamed in fright. They had turned it on so suddenly that even Heather grabbed at my loose sleeve and searched for my hand buried in its folds and had trouble finding it. It sounded like the ghostly cries from our first visit but a hundred times louder and closer. We huddled together while they howled, and we looked around to see how it was affecting the others. No one seemed alarmed except the baby. Everyone began to shuffle forward. We moved out through the hall and then the front door into the rain. The ground glistened underfoot and even the trees wept. Ahead of us the hired mourners tore at their matted hair and cried to the starless heavens. They led us along beside the moat and around the corner of the house and the flames of their tapers sputtered in the wet and some went out.

The chapel door stood open and illuminated the fine rain in a cube of light before it. The mourners led us in through the arched doorway crying all the while; they took places around the walls and stood, tapers in hand, heads bowed, while the family moved into the body of the small chapel and quite filled it. There were chairs and we sat down and waited and looked around. Before the altar was a coffin draped with a banner and with four very large candlesticks, which stood like sentries at each corner.

On one side of me was a large woman whose black skirts overflowed her space and buried my off leg. At the far side of Heather was a boy dressed like a little man in black doublet and hose and with a short cape and a hat with a curling, drooping feather. He had a small sword at his side and it kept poking her in the ankle. Heather stared down at it curiously and he watched Heather watching his sword. I think he let it poke her on purpose.

"Where's your ruff? Where's your cap? You look funny," he whispered hoarsely. "Are you from over the Wall?"

"What wall?" Heather whispered back.

"Why, Hadrian's Wall, of course."

"Never heard of it," said Heather. "And you look pretty funny yourself."

"How so?"

"Well, all the feathers and velvet. I think so anyway, and I'm entitled to an opinion."

They would have gone on, hissing at each other, but I poked her in the ribs and shushed her as a priest with a stubby white ruff moved to the small velvet-covered pulpit and began to speak in an expressionless voice while two altar boys attended him and, when needed, turned the pages of a great book. Heather raised her brows and looked at me. "Latin," I whispered. Her eyes glittered in the light of the many candles, and I saw that her hair was frizzed with the damp. I put a hand up to my own and found it wet. We settled back to listen to his rhythmic words while the woman down front wept softly under her tentlike veil. Only two words did we catch and that was the name "Donald MacDonald." We shivered at the sound of them and looked at each other. This service could be for our own brother!

When the priest finished, four men arose and picked up the coffin. Someone opened a door in the side wall and the men, balancing it between them and led by the priest, shuffled through and began the difficult business of circling with it down the narrow stone steps beyond. The rest of us waited and listened to the click of their

77

heels. But I knew what the crypt was like below. I knew that there was a stone table in the center and shelves waiting in the stone walls, some full, some empty. Around us people cried softly or sniffed into linen.

I whispered into Heather's ear, "Ask your friend with the sword how the heir and his father died."

Heather turned to him and poked him in the side. "How did he die? We didn't hear that over the Wall."

"Skewered like a pig by a highwayman on his way back from London where he'd gone to see some players."

Heather turned to relay it to me. "I heard," I said quickly. "The father?"

Heather poked him again. "His father?"

"Lost in a bog on a Yorkshire moor in a heavy mist only this month past. He was on King James's business in the north."

"That's terrible!" said Heather louder than she realized.

"It's the family curse," he hissed. "This house is cursed and full of ghosts."

"Have you ever seen any?" she demanded.

"No," he said.

"Then you shouldn't say so," said Heather.

"Why not?"

"It's bad news for a house when you come to sell it. So you shouldn't say such things. The owner could sue you."

"Your speech is strange and you are stranger! And I'll say what I like!—and no man says me nay!" and he put his hand to his sword and scowled.

Heather looked interested but I punched her again. The priest and the four tall men returned—I thought they might be MacDonald relatives, they had the noses —and final prayers were said. Then the company arose and murmured to each other and moved out slowly into the rain.

Somehow Heather and the boy managed to stroll out together and I had to follow a step behind as we walked back beside the moat, where some ducks had now assembled in the dark, expecting to be fed. I could only listen as the two ahead of me talked.

"I'm Heather MacDonald," she told him. "What's your name?"

"Angus. I suppose we are cousins."

"Angus? That's the name of a steer —Black Angus. I know a restaurant that serves Black Angus steaks. That's a cut of meat. Our father always orders it."

He looked at her with his mouth open. "I don't understand half of what you say! And I don't think you're polite. If you don't like my name, and I judge that you do not, I might say we have three scullery maids at home all called Heather."

"Are they MacDonalds?"

"Certainly not!"

"Well, I am. I'm family. Could I try your sword?"

"Certainly not!"

"Is that all you can say, 'Certainly not'?"

"Truly, I think you are unmaidenly!"

A man turned to claim the boy. "Come, Angus. We must pay our respects to your Aunt Eleanor," he said and bowed to us solemnly as suited the occasion and we bobbed in return.

"Good-bye, Cousin Angus," said Heather.

"Good-bye, Cousin Heather." He smiled. "I'll look

for you at John MacDonald's house on All Hallow's Eve." He waved and turned to follow his father and the feather in his hat bobbed at his shoulder.

As they moved off with the crowd, I heard the man say, "What odd-looking girls! You do attract them, Angus!"

"They're from beyond the Wall, Father."

"Ah, from the remote Outer Isles! Yes, some of our family continued to filter down attracted by our prosperity. But they should learn to dress properly before they appear in company."

"The little one is very amusing, Father. She has a strange accent and says strange things. She likened me to a cut of meat."

"That *is* strange. What she meant escapes even me, unless it is that you look full-blooded."

They moved up the steps with the rest of the people, past the glistening wet leopards, and disappeared into the lighted doorway of the house. The paid mourners seemed to have melted away into the darkness. There was now just the gurgling of gutters and the splash of water to disturb the silence of the black night as they emptied into the moat.

CHAPTER SEVEN

So MARGARET WAS GONE AND THE MAID DIDN'T EVEN know of her. Heather didn't bring back the doll; I think now she would have fancied Angus's small sword. At one point I thought of bringing back the stub of a taper, but a hand-dipped candle of one age is much like that of another and would prove nothing.

Next morning, as Mother brushed and tied back our hair—first Heather's and then mine, she said, "Your hair seems damp. Did you get it wet in the shower last night?"

We glanced at each other. Well, we weren't trying to keep any secrets from the family; we wanted them to know, so I said firmly, "We went to Austwick Manor again. We wanted to bring something back to prove to you that it was all true, Margaret's doll, perhaps. It was raining hard."

The hairbrush in Mother's hand stopped in midair. "George!" she shouted.

Father emerged from the bathroom with a face covered with foam and the razor in his hand. "Yes, Mary?"

"The girls' hair is damp! They say they were out in the rain last night!"

"It didn't rain last night."

"It did at the manor," I said.

"Hard enough to put the mourners' candles out," said Heather.

The foam was drying fast on father's face. "Tell me," he ordered.

We told him, taking turns. Heather remembered how everything looked, even the pattern on the banner over the casket, also the style of the little black caps on the ladies' heads and their long black veils, and of course, I remembered Angus's sword that kept jabbing her in the leg, and what everybody said, like the woman saying, "Where's your ruffs? What's your maid thinking of to turn you out so. For shame! She needs shaking up, that one!" and the mourner who shouted, "Did you bring your black clouts?"

"Who was the funeral for?" Mother asked in a small voice.

"The son and heir—and his name was Donald, too. And they told us his father had just gone before, 'lost in a Yorkshire bog on King James's business in the north.' It must have been one of the alternate generations like the curse said. The woman who put us into black thought so too. She said, 'It's the soothsayer's words come true! That's what it is!' "

Mother finished with us in a hurry. "Run along, girls. You'll be late for school," she said.

We left, but noticed that she was staring straight in front of her, still holding the brush. Father went and laid his lathery face against hers and said something soothing. She said fiercely, "It doesn't work, you know! I dared them to show me! It's just their imaginations because it doesn't work!"

We continued down the porch steps and turned up the street. I was sorry to worry them, but they had to believe us and do something to save Don!

About this time Father began a serious study of the household accounts and the journals and soon became besotted with them (Mother's words). He wanted to transcribe and publish them. He brought to our house a student from the University to help him, someone interested in the period and who "knew a thing or two" about it, Father said. The student's name was Pringle. He was about nineteen and had thick glasses and always seemed to be wearing his roommate's moldy sweater that was two sizes too big for him. They spent evenings deciphering the Elizabethan writing and passed the sheets to mother to type up. It became a project with the three of them.

Don was only mildly interested, but then he had homework and so did we. We three had to study at the kitchen table because they had the dining table covered with dictionaries and source books. And they wouldn't allow any television either. We were supposed to concentrate on our work as they were doing on theirs. Heather and I would pick up phrases they puzzled over and sometimes we knew what was meant and would shout and tell them, and then there would be a surprised silence in the dining room. Pringle was fascinated by us. Mother was not.

Sometimes I hung around where the transcribing was going on, and it amused Pringle to point out the strange lettering and how the one that looked like a *u* was really an *n* and the *s* was an *f*. If I remembered this and went slowly, I could make out the writing myself. Heather said she couldn't read anybody's script—even

Mother's notes on the refrigerator door—and wouldn't even try. But I went at it like a puzzle, one word at a time, and with practice it became easier. Pringle told me that in those days no two people spelled alike, so you just guessed at what they meant and tried to make sense out of it. I said I wished spelling was like that today. Anyway, Pringle, with his lank hair hanging in his eyes, thought it great fun and would have worked at it all night if mother hadn't sent him home at midnight.

Pringle was always hungry: he ate whatever was offered and dropped crumbs in the research, which upset Father for he had a great respect for books. Sometimes on weekends, Pringle had dinner with us and then he really got down to serious eating. It was at the table one evening that Heather said to Don indignantly in reply to something, "Do you think I'm a great gowk?"

"A what?" said Don

Mother smiled. "Is that the latest word this week on the school ground?"

Pringle looked up from his plate. "Gowk. (1) the cuckoo. (2) A half-witted person; a fool. Scottish and north English. 1605" Then he tucked into his food again. Mother looked at Heather sharply—so did Father. They didn't ask where she'd heard it; they seemed afraid to. After one glance at Mother's face, Father wanted to drop the subject but Pringle grinned. "She possibly heard us transcribing it—although I don't remember a passage using the word, do you, George?" Father did not reply.

Heather answered Pringle. "We didn't get it from you or the journals. It was what the maid said to one of the paid mourners squatting on the stairs at the Manor.

She said, 'Move, you great gowk! Can't you see you're in the way of your betters!'—that was us," said Heather with satisfaction. "We were family. They were just hired weepers and wailers for the occasion."

Don muttered, "More of the same," and rolled his eyes to heaven.

But Pringle listened with interest. Father was plainly worried; he didn't want to upset Mother in her condition. Mother just stared at the vegetable dish a long time as if she was considering buying it and then said brightly, "More cottage pie, Pringle?" Pringle was delighted to have more and the bad moment passed.

Father and Pringle had begun on the first book and Mother had typed out the opening. I read it out loud to Heather.

"Today, being the 21st day of the seventh month of the year 1540, I, Donald Mac-Donald, one time of Northumberland and before that of the Isles, did take over the manor house of Austwick the gift of Her Royal Highness the Princess Mary Tudor. My lady wife my son Donald my female child Margaret and the twin infants Ian and Rory took possession and were much pleased with our good fortune. The twins being soon of crawling age were put in a safe room with gate and their wet-nurse to watch over them my young daughter the corner room with her nursemaid my heir an excellent big room in the East wing with a schoolroom attached and a closet for his tutor and we

*took the large chamber over the great hall
with a fireplace and a very fine carved
mantel. . . ."*

I read all Mother had typed, but it only went to the
end of the first year of their life in the Manor. Heather
had to know why you'd keep a tutor in a closet and
other things, but I didn't know. Pringle came in as I laid
the papers down.

"Well, what do you think of it, Hillary?" he asked

I liked Pringle. He always treated me with respect.
"It'll get more interesting," I said. "Tell me when you
come to the gift of the doll. Margaret told us the Princess had 'gifted her with a poppet on her birthing day'
when she was a child—and we saw it."

Pringle stared down at me through his thick lenses
and said he would do just that!

He worked like a fiend pushing the transcribing of
the first section. I think he wanted to see if those items
were mentioned. Anyway, one day when I returned
from the playground, Mother and Father and Pringle
looked up from their notes and stared at me as I came in.
I knew at once they had found mention of the doll and
my heart leaped with excitement.

They had, but instead of congratulating us for
being right, Father said quietly, "You must admit, Hillary, you have learned to pick your way through this
difficult script. You could have dipped into the book and
read these details and used them."

My smile faded. "Use them? You mean lied
about it?"

They didn't answer. I ran up to my room and threw
myself down on my bed and cried bitterly.

86

Mother came up later and took me in her arms but she couldn't find anything to say. I heard Don come home in Charlie's screeching car and, a few minutes later, go whistling down the hall to his room. The memory of that sad woman under the black veil stayed with me. I wanted to cry out, "I'm so afraid for my brother! Our father died a strange death! You always said so, Mother!" but I couldn't. I would only distress her and we had been warned against that. I never felt so alone.

In the days that followed, they encountered other things in the household accounts that we had mentioned. One list of expenses was very interesting but I did not point it out. It went like this:

1s. for sheepskin rug for my daughter Margaret's chamber.

1s. for repairs to latch of livery cupboard.

20 pounds 10s. for dove-colored dress for my wife.

18 pounds for blue velvet dress for my daughter Margaret.

20 pounds for new doublets and hose for twins and heir.

1s. a head for extra beaters for Royal hunt . . . 15 beaters all told.

10 pounds for French wine for head table.

2 pounds for ale etc for attendants.

2 pounds for performers and mummers . . .

It went on and on itemizing all the foods for the banquet and many were those we had talked about.

As these things came to light, I pretended not to be interested. Let them stare. But they still said to each other that I was a clever child and must have deciphered bits in later journals and passed it on to Heather. I got to the point that if anyone asked me what time it was, I'd say, "Why ask me! You'd never believe me!" Don said I was a sorehead and mother that "it quite spoiled my nature," and of course, Heather suffered too, for "keeping up the silly game."

Father was excited when he found the first mention of the building of the Tudor house model. "Listen to this!" he cried. "On the fifth of May, 1551," MacDonald writes, "My daughter Margaret on going to Spain was there stricken with so severe a sickness for her old home that she could neither eat nor sleep with her new husband without tears. On learning this, I therefore ordered to have built a model of that portion of the house she loved the best to be outfitted with divers furnishings as were accustomed to be in it and to be sent in care of a ship's master to Spain."

They were all thrilled on reading this but Heather and I sulked a little knowing they hadn't believed us about Margaret not wanting to go to Spain. From that date MacDonald wrote often of the progress of the model with wages paid to artisans who worked on it, the silversmiths and the furniture makers and the women who sewed. Everything was listed in the account book for that year.

But mother's thrill was not as great as that of the others. I would look up to find her eyes on me—or on Heather. Then one day when we came in from school, we saw that they had changed the dolls again. "That woman in black depressed me," Mother said. "She looked so alone in that big chamber."

Heather cried, "But she was very beautiful! I liked her!"

"Lonely, just lonely," Mother murmured as if to herself and walked away to the kitchen.

We peered in through the small diamond windows. We saw another assortment of dolls occupying the house, all in different dress. Both the women and the men were very fancy, no more ruffs, but wide, flat-lace collars that came right out to the points of their shoulders. The men wore silk hosiery and full knickers of satin with bows on the outside and wide frills falling over their knees. They also had flowing ribbons on the top of their sleeves and curling hair to their shoulders and large brimmed hats with plumes. The women had tight bodices and full skirts of pale silk and big sleeves. They were very pretty and had bunches of tight ringlets over their ears and looked like spaniels.

But we said nothing more and went up to our room to change into play clothes. "Mother is worried," I said and Heather nodded. "I think the thing to do is involve Don."

"Fat chance! He won't even listen."

"But they would believe him! They think we have too much imagination. I guess we have and now it's working against us. Well, I'll think about it. I'll think of something."

I thought about it all the rest of the day and by evening I had a plan. I told Heather and she thought it might work. It all depended on our brother being a heavy sleeper—which he was and very hard to awaken: he would lean against the tile wall of the shower and go on sleeping until the water ran so cold that it woke him up—or until Father hauled him out—by then there was no hot water left for anyone else. Mother excused him because he was a growing boy. He had grown four inches during the last year, she reminded us, and there was all that gym work and karate lessons and judo and soccer and cycling and being an editor of the Annual. . . . He needed his sleep, she insisted.

"What can we lose?" said Heather. "They won't believe us, but maybe they'll believe the Rightful Heir." (She still could not forgive Don for inheriting Austwick Manor.)

So at midnight, we got out of bed quietly—for these nights Mother was sleeping lightly—put on our robes and went to Don's room. "Close the door," I whispered, "in case Mother hears us." I found his tartan flannel robe and his mukluks. I shook him, but very carefully, and spoke gently. "Don, get up! We need you . . . !" He didn't move. I was afraid to shake him any harder because we had to be careful with him these days. Ever since he had been taking karate lessons, you had to be cautious how you approached him. His reflexes were being trained to instant reaction, he said. If anyone came on him unexpectedly from the rear, he'd likely swing fast and give him a chop. So now I talked soothingly and made no threatening moves. I was tempted to say there was an earthquake or a flood or something and that we had to evacuate, but I had been warned never to cry wolf. "Get up this instant!" I said and tried to sound like Mother giving out with orders. I patted him again but with gentle love pats. He floated up to the surface of sleep and muttered something that sounded like, "Wasser . . . wasser . . . wasser. . . ." I pulled his feet over the side of the bed and pushed his mukluks on.

I sat him up carefully and got his arms into the sleeves of his dressing gown and did my best to button it up. He still muttered, "What's this? What's going on . . . ?" but seemed to sleep again before I could answer, so I just pulled him up gently and steered him to the door.

Heather had been listening for Mother, but now she opened it quickly and let us through. We led him, still asleep, down to the dining room, and we each took one of his hands and stood for a moment facing the manor house.

"It didn't work for three the last time," Heather said anxiously.

"But Mother hasn't MacDonald blood in her veins! Don has! So have we!"

"I hope you're right. What can we lose?"

This night there was no moon to shine through our big bay window. It was dark out and foggy. Even our friendly street lamp wore a fuzzy halo. The model was a dark block, and featureless. "Ready?" I whispered.

Heather nodded. We stepped forward and pulled our brother after us. My heart was beating wildly. Would it work with him? I wondered, suddenly doubting my theory. If it didn't, I didn't know what else we could do to prove it all! Don muttered something that sounded like "Wasser matter . . . ? I wanna go back to sleep. . . ." but we clung to him and drew him forward.

Then suddenly I felt the gravel crunch under my foot again! It was working! "We're there!" I cried. "We're there!"

Heather's whisper was like an echo. "We're there!"

But it was a wild scene we came on. The wind howled around the dark house and the rain pelted down.

About twenty horses that were tied in the gravel approach strained at their bridles, whinnied and struggled to turn their rumps into the storm; their manes were tossed around their ears and their tails lashed them just as the tree boughs lashed the side of the house. The rain gusted and was blown almost parallel to the ground. I clutched the collar of my robe close to my neck and the skirt whipped my bare legs. Like the horses, I turned sideways to take the blast on my rear while strands of hair stung my face and eyes.

Heather leaned across Don and shouted, "The front door is open! Listen!"

Then, to our astonishment, men in steel helmets charged out of the house carrying bundles of bed clothes; things fell from them and rolled on the ground—teapots, sugar bowls, spoons. The silver bounced and flashed although the wind drowned out all but an occasional clink and tinkle of metal on gravel. The men were in high spirits. They clutched their ungainly loot, pulled themselves into their saddles clumsily with it and took off—only one horse remained. One of the men looked back and yelled, "Where's Jack?" and another shouted, "He'll catch up! Away! . . . before someone comes . . . !" The wind took their voices as they disappeared around the curve of the drive.

A voice spoke somewhere above my ear. "What's going on?"

I looked up. Don was scowling after the soldiers. He looked bewildered.

"We told you!" I shouted back. "We told you!"

"What's going on?" he insisted.

"I don't know! Everything looks different somehow!"

"Thieving soldiers!" he cried. "And there's still one in there! That's our house he's looting!"

He pulled away from us and charged over the short bridge and into the house. We followed after, afraid to be left behind, yet afraid to go in.

Everything was in disarray, the furniture overturned, things dragged from room to room. We heard angry voices coming from above. Don went up the staircase two at a time, past the leopard on the newel post and the suit of armor on the half-turn and on up. We pounded after him, tripping over bedding, for the soldiers had been dragging that away when they had found something that they fancied better. But there was a fight going on—a screaming, shouting, banging and crashing fight in the great chamber. Don stopped at the doorway panting and stared. We peered in under his elbows. Two men were fighting: the sword blades flashed and sang and their heels clanged and slid on the polished plank floors.

We watched and dodged as the fight advanced and retreated. Don edged into the room warily. One of the swordsmen was young—about twenty; he was dressed in silks and his hair was long. The other was much older and grizzled. He had on a coarse suit, woolen stockings and shoes with big buckles. He had a wide leather bandolier from shoulder to waist and a wide white collar, none too clean. He had on the steel helmet of a soldier and it glinted dully in the dusky chamber. He hacked away at the boy and more than once got him up against the wall. They were aware of us, but they couldn't afford to take their eyes from each other. It was at one of these times, when both swordsmen had the other held immobile for a second, that we saw the young man's profile. There, once again, was the nose with the high bridge!

"Stop!" Don cried. "Stop! Hold!"

The young man's eyes barely blinked sideways. Immediately the soldier laughed a harsh laugh, leaped forward like lightning and flicked the boy with his sword so that the blood spurted from his arm.

It happened too fast for me to follow. Just as the man recovered and was about to plunge his sword through the boy, Don seized a stool and hurled it. It caught the man on the back of the head and knocked his helmet flying. His sword arced through the air and fell with a clatter, and Don was on him at once. With what looked like no effort at all, he seized the man's arm, twisted, and he flew across the room and landed hard against the corner of a great chest and lay there stunned.

Meanwhile, blood was pouring from the young man's arm. He clutched it and his fingers ran red. "Who are you?" he demanded. "Did you come with them?"

"No, we just arrived," I said. "We saw the soldiers ride away and then heard your shouts up here."

He looked puzzled. "Someone come to visit my sisters? Don't you know it's dangerous to be on the roads now? The Roundheads are ravaging the district."

"We didn't know," I said. "We're MacDonalds. This is my brother Donald and my sister Heather. I'm Hillary. Who are you?"

"I'm a Donald also, 'Donald Dhu,' they call me, to tell me from some of the others of the same name. I'm in your debt, Cousin Donald."

"No. If I hadn't taken your attention by shouting—"

"If you hadn't thrown the stool I'd be dead. I'm a student, not a swordsman."

"You'd better let us look at that arm."

"They got a good haul—and they'll be back to look for this man when he doesn't turn up."

"We'll fix that. We'll put him on his horse and perhaps it will follow the others."

It seemed like a good idea. We turned the man over. There was a discolored mark on his temple where I thought he might have hit the corner of the chest. "You've killed him, Don!" I gasped.

Don felt the spot carefully. "No," he said. "It's not soft. It's a stain of some kind, a blemish, maybe just dirt."

I was relieved and saw that my brother was right. The mark was the color of a dark freckle and the shape of a small horseshoe and definitely not dried mud, as it didn't brush off.

We tried to carry him to the stair head but he was too heavy for us. Donald Dhu's arm bled too much and he fell away clutching it.

"I'll take care of this," said Don. "You see to his arm, Hillary."

I led Donald Dhu to a chair while Don rolled the soldier onto a small rug and then towed it to the stair head quite easily over the polished oak floor and bumped him down the stairs. We could hear him in the lower hall and then some minutes later out in the driveway below the window as he shouted to the horse and sent it galloping after the others. I suppose he must have got the idea from TV but it came in handy.

He returned breathless. "I had to lead the horse to

lower ground and get the fellow on the bridge above and drop him into the saddle. I tied him on and slapped the horse on the rump and it took off. He's still out cold."

"I hope he freezes," said Donald Dhu.

We looked at him and then at each other. My brother said carefully, "I meant, 'He was still unconscious.' "

"Ah, 'senseless.' Good!"

"Get your shirt off and let's look at that arm."

It was a nasty cut, deep and open like a mouth. Heather looked away. I wanted to. It needed to be stitched and we had nothing to dress it with. "We need bandages." I said.

Donald Dhu looked pale. "The linen press in the hall. . . . Old sheets. . . . My mother hoards them for such occasions."

I went out to the massive piece of furniture that stood on the landing and opened its doors. On the shelves within was all the household linen neatly folded. On the top shelf, one that I could barely reach, was a card in curly writing that said, "Linen—Outworn." I pulled one down. It was a half sheet thin but clean, and I tore off strips and rolled them up. But how to disinfect the wound! That's what bothered me. "I think we'll need hot water," I said as I went back into the great chamber.

"Kitchen," he murmured. His eyes were closed now.

I was going to go downstairs with Don but he said, "The soldiers might still come back. I'll go. I've bolted the front door." He went off on the run.

I got Donald Dhu to lie down on the disarranged canopied bed and I put a linen pad over the wound and tried to hold it closed. It was like tending my own brother—he was so like him, only darker. Heather said nothing, just stared around the wrecked chamber and began absently to pick up things, jars of pomade, patch boxes, a hand mirror; she righted chairs that were almost too heavy for her to move and replaced cushions.

Don returned and we bathed the wound. "The fire was still burning in the grate and the pots are all hot," he said as we bandaged the arm tightly. "The servants must have only just left."

Donald Dhu murmured, "I was at my college at Oxford. I heard there was trouble in our shire and hurried home. I met one of our stablemen rushing off. He told me the family had been warned to get out. Cromwell's men were approaching and Cromwell has no love for the likes of us. But the servants should have stayed. He had nothing on them, but they bolted and left the soldiers to make free with the house. . . . And here was I, only just arrived, when the troop came riding up."

"Surely you didn't try to hold off twenty men!" said Don.

"No. I hid until I thought they were all gone, then ventured out and walked right into the last straggler and his sword."

"You look faint," I said.

"Perhaps it's hunger. I came at fast gallop. I supped last night—not since."

"I'll see what I can find," Don said.

He went downstairs again and young MacDonald lay quietly with his eyes closed for a minute, then he said, "You say you came to see my sisters?"

I said quickly, "Like you, our timing was bad."

"You shouldn't have been abroad! This is no time to travel. Where is your home?"

"The islands," I said again.

97

"A long journey indeed! Perhaps the news hasn't yet reached there, but times are very bad in England."

"Yes," I murmured, but I didn't know why they were so bad.

"Your sister is very quiet. The fighting must have frightened the child."

"It frightened me," I said.

"And there might well be more. There are still things of value in the house. They'll be back to clean it out."

Don brought up a pan of soup and four bowls. He doled it out with a ladle—hot barley soup with leeks and carrots. We put pillows behind our cousin and helped him manage his spoon. He looked around thoughtfully and said, "I'm unused to this room. Mine is across the hall. It was too small to swing a sword in. We worked our way in here by common consent."

He dozed off then. We stirred up the fire and threw on another log and sat close to it, almost inside the fender, while the wind howled around the house and buffeted the eaves.

"What are we going to do," said Heather voicing what was in all our minds.

"What usually happens?" Don asked.

I was aware that he was acknowledging our stories now, but I said nothing to point this up. "I don't know exactly. We usually wake up in our own beds."

"We can't leave him like this. That's a nasty wound and if they come back, he'll be helpless."

We sat on in silence, poking the fire, checking the bed to see that he was all right. Toward morning the wind died down and a dark and dismal day broke. You

98

couldn't call it sunrise, for there was no sun, just a lessening of the dark and always the perpetual rain.

In the new quiet, I went to the window, leaned on the cushioned seat there and looked out. For a minute I thought there was a sunrise after all, but it was something burning beyond the woods. I called the others. Donald Dhu heard us and awakened and asked what it was and we told him that there was a fire beyond the park.

"The Abbey!" he groaned. "They're having their fun knocking out stained glass. I hear they took out the great window at the cathedral. "They'll be back!"

"Then we have to have a plan," I said. "Either we have to get away from here or we have to hold them off!"

"Too many of them," he said heavily, "and they can always send for more."

"Then we have to hide as you did and hope they go away. The priest hole," I said. "We can use the priest hole!"

He sat up and stared at me. "How do you know about that? No one but family knows about that. That's where I hid. But no one outside the family knows about that!"

My brother said quickly, "Never mind. We can stock it with food. . . . Let's go! Supplies first. Come on, Heather. I need you." Heather, glad for something to do, rushed off with him.

I said, "You'll need blankets."

"The chest there. . . ." He pointed to the foot of the bed, but he was still looking at me curiously.

I got out several blankets and looked in the clothes

press and found a splendid fur-lined cloak and hauled it out. "How do we reach the attic?" I asked him.

"The east wing."

The model had no wings—only the front section with the main entrance. "You'll have to lead the way," I said. I got him up and put the fur cape around him and he hesitated a moment to snatch up some writing materials and a book, then he led me down and through the back. Don and Heather joined us at the kitchen door. They each carried a heavy basket of bread and meat and other supplies and we followed Donald Dhu along another hall, up more stairs and then up some very narrow ones hidden in a closet, and found ourselves under the eaves. Ahead of us I saw the great brick chimney as wide as the end of the house—wider and deeper than it needed to be, I well knew!

Donld Dhu went to the far side of it, felt around, and we heard a latch click. Don had to help him swing the false front out. It moved forward on invisible wheels only a foot or two and there was space enough for us all to slip in behind. The room was tiny, about four feet wide but over twenty feet or so long. The real chimney was there against the outside wall and the bricks were warm, although the roof above, with its exposed slate tiles, was icy cold. There was the frame of a cot with a mattress, a *prie dieu*, a long bench, a pail and nothing else.

I quickly made the bed with the clothes I had brought up and Don arranged a jug of water and a tankard on the stool beside it and hung the baskets on hooks provided to keep them out of the way of mice. Heather found several peepholes in the outside walls, some looking forward to the driveway, where puddles shone like dull mirrors in the early morning light, some to the side, where the flames of the burning abbey and one or two other buildings lit up the gloomy sky. There was even a hole that looked back into the attic.

Before he lay down again, Donald Dhu looked through the hole at the distant flames. "The abbey first and now the grand big house of the Marples' going up! I wish no bad luck on them, they're good friends, but there's much of value to be looted in that house! They'll have good pickings there! It might just keep them occupied and away from us."

"There's a third fire on the far left."

"That's the Shannons'. God help them! Is the whole countryside to be ravaged, then!" He went back to the cot and lay back with his good arm across his eyes to hide his grief. "I wonder where my family is this night," he murmured. "God grant they be safe!"

"Where would they go?"

"To France or the Low Countries perhaps 'til better times come to England. If they're alive they'll get word to me."

He seemed to sleep after that. We sat on the long oak bench, taking turns at the peephole that looked on the carriage way.

Time passed. It seemed we were no sooner watching the daybreak paling the sky, then it was darkening again in a short winter's day. Don looked at the other Donald on the cot, who was perhaps only four years older than he was. "The nose isn't so bad—distinguished, I think."

Heather sniffed. "It is on him."

"What are we to do?" I asked. "Can we go and leave him?"

"Hardly," Don said. "But if we did, could we get back to him?"

"I don't know," I said. "That hasn't been proved out. You see, Mother kept changing the dolls, and each time we came back, time seemed to have moved on."

"Tell me about it."

"We tried to and you'd never listen," snapped Heather.

"I'm listening now!" he snapped back. "So tell me!"

"Well, when we first came, we met Margaret Mac-Donald and there was much talk of Mary Tudor. She was just driving away as we arrived. Mother thought we had imagined it all and removed the Margaret doll and all the others. The next time we came, many years seemed to have passed and there was a funeral going on, the son and heir of that time had just been killed and they said his father had only just been buried, too. You see, that follows the curse laid down by the soothsayer under Mary Tudor. The man who was in the dungeon, remember?"

"And what period was this?"

"I don't know but when we asked after Margaret, they didn't know who we meant and the room belonged to the son whose funeral it was. But the curse said every second generation."

Don thought it over. "I believe a generation is figured at thirty years more or less."

"So this must be another jump?" I asked.

"No mistaking this period. He's used the word 'Roundheads' several times."

"And he was almost killed. . . ." said Heather.

"Do you believe in the curse?" he asked me.

"I don't know, Don," I said avoiding his eyes.

"Well, I don't," he said. "Exactly what was the curse anyway?"

"The seer was going around saying things about Mary Tudor. He said she'd be known in history as Bloody Mary—that she'd sit on the throne and be followed by the daughter of a trollop and die unhappy. MacDonald ordered him to stop and threw him in the dungeon when he refused. That was when the seer let loose with the curse."

Don looked thoughtful. "It's true Mary was called Bloody Mary, and it's true she inherited the throne when her half-brother Edward died, and it's true she was followed by Elizabeth, whose mother wasn't thought much of by some people. And I think Mary died childless and unhappy."

"So it all came true?"

"Well, the curse could well have been dreamed up after the fact—after it had all happened. It's easy to make up a story about something after it's all happened."

Margaret did say that perhaps her father had made it all up to entertain them on a cold night. . . . But wait! She could afford to laugh because it hadn't happened yet! *Later*, it came true! So she hadn't told the tale after the fact. I didn't have a chance to argue the point because Don's thoughts had moved on.

"The thing is, can we chance leaving him now and getting back to see how he is? I've got an exam tomorrow —not that I'd mind missing it—but what excuse could I give? 'Excuse me, I had to stop a sword fight between a Cavalier and a Roundhead.' "

I said thoughtfully, "We've always told the family about our visits—trying to make them believe. If we say nothing this time Mother might not change the dolls again. I think that's what does it, changing the dolls—but I don't know for sure. We could chance it."

We continued to sit on the hard oak bench and think about it. There were long silences. Don slept a little and I must have too, because when I opened my eyes again there was my very own rose wallpaper staring me in the face with the rhinoceros poster Heather insisted on hanging and there was Heather herself sitting up in the next bed staring at me.

CHAPTER EIGHT

"WE'RE BACK," SHE SAID. "SO IS DON. I CHECKED HIS room."

I nodded. "Remember, we don't talk about it this time."

"You can count on me."

Later, we glanced at Don across the breakfast table. He gave a little nod of the head and went on eating. Meanwhile, Father talked cheerily about the progress of the transcribing. He said, "Girls, you must remember we're dealing with the passage of over four hundred years in these journals. You must be prepared to read of all kinds of things happening to the family. That's life."

"Of course, Father," I said.

"Some of your favorite characters will disappear from the pages and you must accept this. That's in the nature of things."

Heather stopped eating her french toast and looked at him. "You've found out something more about Margaret, haven't you? She's dead, isn't she?"

I saw Father glance at Mother quickly. But he said calmly, "Yes, we came on it in last night's transcribing.

She died quite young—in the next year as a matter of fact. She would have been just seventeen."

"In Spain—of homesickness?"

"It said 'of a Spanish Tertiary Fever.' MacDonald wrote very sadly of it in the journal. She never saw the model of her old home. She died before it was completed and sent off."

We were all silent. The family was watching us and we knew it. Heather's eyes were bright but she blinked back her tears and didn't cry. I felt a hard lump in my throat.

Mother looked anxious. She said. "As your father said, you have to take the long view of history and not get sentimentally attached to . . . to . . . people. . . ." She ended lamely, I thought.

"It's only that she didn't want to go to Spain! When we first saw her, she was crying because she didn't want to go. I think we cheered her up a little. . . . I wonder if she made Cherries Jubilee for her new husband. I hope I got it right."

"Excuse me," said Heather and left the table. I followed her, and after a decent interval, Don came up to our room looking for us.

"What are they saying?" I asked quietly.

"Mother is still worried to death about you. They're talking about sending you both to a psychiatrist."

"Are they going to?"

"They're remembering how far Miss Martin got with you. Then there's the expense—double, because there's two of you."

"So?"

"The conclusion is always that you're going

through a phase and will grow out of it. That's Mother's security blanket. 'You'll grow out of it.' "

"And now there's you."

"Well, they don't know that yet."

"Oh, they won't talk about a psychiatrist for you! You're too solid a citizen. Ask any teacher at school!" I said, annoyed.

"You're no slouch yourself at school—you and Heather. What are we going to do about Donald Dhu?"

"Collect things to take back tonight."

"Is that possible?"

"If Heather brought back a comfit, we ought to be able to take in some sticking plaster. What have you got that we can use?"

"Bandages—some pain pills the doctor gave me after the auto accident and the surgery."

"Bring them. I know where there's some surgical powder the vet gave us for the cat."

"For the cat!?" said Heather.

"A wound is a wound."

"Bring it," said Don. "But I wish we could get good advice."

"Well, we can't. We can't get him shots or anything like that."

"I wish we hadn't had to leave him. I'm worried."

"I wonder what he'll think when he wakes up and finds we're gone," said Heather. "He'll think we deserted him, that's what."

"He'll hope we went for help."

"Against the soldiers? There isn't any! They're in power right now," said Don.

"Perhaps he can escape and follow his family to

the continent. We must help him get away! But I'm worried about his wound. It needed a doctor."

The day seemed never to end. Mother remarked on our mood and asked if we felt all right. Don had it easier because he had a lot of business at school and that kept him occupied. At last dinner was over, a silent meal, and everyone separated to do what he chose to do—Father to push the transcription for an hour or two, Mother to type a few pages for him. We went to our room early and settled down to wait for midnight.

When the house quieted at last, we got up and awakened Don. He alerted much better this time, because it was on his mind, I guess, and we didn't have to lead him out asleep, thank goodness. So, with our robe pockets stuffed with bandages and sticking plaster, and with the pain medication, which had once been given to Don by our very own doctor, and the surgical powder from the vet—the cat had healed quickly with its help— we crept down to the dining room, took hands and faced the model.

"Have we got everything?"

"Yes. Are you ready?"

"Hurry," said Heather. "Let's go!"

We took one step toward the edge of the rug. Suddenly a voice behind us shouted. "Stop! What are you doing?"

We swung around. Mother was standing in the hall doorway. She put her hand to the switch and the lights blazed on. "George!" she shouted over her shoulder.

Father came running, his hair all on end, his eyes only half-open from sleep. "What is it, Mary? Is it time?" He was thinking about the baby.

"Look!" she cried pointing at us. "I heard a noise

and got up, they've got Don into it now! I won't have it! How can they worry me like this!" She began to cry.

"What's going on here!" shouted Father, now fully awake.

"Donald Dhu is wounded and we have to get back and help him," I said, my voice quivering in a way that I could do nothing about.

"That's right, Father," Don said. "We visited the Manor last night and he's badly wounded and in the priest hole! Look, we're taking in bandages and things!"

Mother was horrified. She cried again. "They're mad! And now they've made Don mad! Go to your rooms at once, all of you! How can you do this to me!"

"We have to help him—he's hurt!" I yelled desperately. "Please, don't stop us!"

But Mother was already pushing Heather toward the door and Father was steering Don in the same direction. Everybody was yelling, I, louder than anybody. Somebody took hold of me and I shook them off and screamed that I had to get back, that they mustn't stop me. I don't remember anything after that except dim noise and shouting. I don't know what happened. What I remember next was waking up with a head like a boiled owl and Heather peering down at me from the side of my bed.

"Are you awake?" she whispered. I grunted. "We've been waiting for you to get up. I'll go and tell them."

Before I could stop her—for I seemed strangely slow-moving and my eyes badly focused—she had darted out. When I opened them again, she was carrying a breakfast tray with orange juice and toast and all the rest. The boiled egg had a little woolen cozy on it to keep it hot, and I suppose it was meant to amuse me, for it always had made me laugh before. Don came in after her and closed the door.

"What happened?" I asked them. "I can't seem to remember."

"You had a fit of hysterics and scared the daylights out of them."

"Hysterics?" I repeated, bewildered.

"You fell to the floor and kicked and screamed and drummed with your heels and raised holy Ned. They sent for the doctor and he came and gave you a shot and knocked you out. Mother collapsed and Father and the doctor had both of you on their hands for a while. You sure gave everyone a fright."

I was certainly surprised. Hysterics? Did that mean a tantrum? I didn't know. Waldo, the kid on the corner, had tantrums. One day I saw him have one on his front lawn. His mother turned the hose full on him and he sputtered and yelled to a gurgling stop. He looked pretty silly, and I was embarrassed to have seen it. Well, they hadn't turned a hose on me. Was it only because there wasn't one handy in the dining room? Now I was embarrassed for myself. I didn't want to look at them. "What's happening?" I mumbled, my eyes on my plate of toast. "Where's Mother?"

"Packing."

"Packing?"

"They're taking us to the lake."

"The lake? But it's the wrong time of year and . . . ! It'll be cold at the lake! And it's only Thursday!"

"Father's taking today off and Friday and Monday, too. Pringle is coming with us to help out. They're packing supplies now."

"We're going to miss school?"

110

"Seems that way."

I thought, They must be desperate to do this! "But why?"

"They've decided we need a change of scene or something."

Father came bustling in. "Up you get, Hillary! Feeling chipper? Good! Put on warm clothing. We're going to the lake. We're going to climb the mountain behind the cottage and go boating and fish and hike. We've never been there at this time of year. It'll be different."

"It'll be cold," said Heather glumly.

"You'll like it. It's bracing," said Father in a tone that meant there would be no further discussion.

An hour later, we were on the road up the Island, three in the front seat, three in the back with our feet on cold tanks and hampers, extra coats and rain gear. Pringle sat with Don and me in the back; Heather was in front in the middle on the hump. Father was trying to be cheerful and chatty as he drove, but the only response he got was from Pringle. Mother was silent and, of course, the rest of us were. We had reason to be. They had taken us away so we couldn't get back to help Donald Dhu! I felt miserable. I know the others did too.

It was drizzling when we got to Grandmother's old cottage by the lake. It was locked for the season, with shutters on all windows that had to be opened. When we got in at last, it was terribly cold with a damp kind of cold that went to the bones, but father brushed aside our complaints and set us to collecting wood for a fire. The activities, he said, would get our blood flowing.

And so began our long, chilly weekend, which was supposed to knock all fantasies out of our heads. Mother was left to sit over the fire, with Pringle to fetch and carry for her—she was now moving around clumsily—while Father led us on a climbing expedition to the top of the four-thousand-foot mountain behind the cottage, where we collapsed panting, too tired to enjoy the view. Don was in good condition, of course, but he wasn't in any mood to enter into the spirit of things as laid down by Father. He took us on a long hike, too. Under a heavy sky we plowed through dead bracken soggy with a week's rain and stepped into mud holes that tugged at our rubber boots when we tried to lift our feet. On the third day we were allowed to rest up, as Father took Mother in the car to get more supplies. Pringle was left in charge of us.

"We're not going to walk another step," I told him. "I don't care what instructions they left you with!"

"Relax," he said and grinned. "How about getting out the boat and exploring the lake?"

"It's been explored," said Don. "Our mother's grandfather explored it and all the land around. He owned everything in sight. He logged it off and divided it and sold it, acre by acre. What's to explore?"

"Well, you can show me around. I'm a guest."

"If you'll do your own rowing," I said. "We're bushed!"

Even getting out the boat was exhausting; it was heavy and I was immediately suspicious that even that chore had been planned by father to wear us down further and make us "too tired to dream any silly dreams about Austwick Manor." But we dragged it out of the boathouse and got it launched at last—by common consent letting Pringle do most of the work, for we thought him allied with our parents on this, and it served him right if he had to heave it around with a minimum of help from us. We climbed in and let Pringle take the oars; Heather perched on the prow, huddled in a hooded coat made out of a three-point Hudson Bay blanket, which had once belonged to me and which I had grown out of—and would likely be kept in mothballs until the new baby Rebecca could use it. Don and I slouched in the stern, where we had no intention of doing anything more energetic than occasionally dip our fingers in the icy water and shudder. All around the lake the second growth fir and cedar grew down to the water line; the quiet was as oppressive as the damp air.

We moved out from our landing with only the clunk of the oarlocks raising echoes on the deserted lake and a splash when Pringle caught a crab, for he was no great oarsman. At the far end, a year-round resident who liked solitude was clearing his land; he was burning out a stump and the smoke from it moved off slowly in the heavy air like a gray chiffon scarf caught among the trees. No one spoke. We all had our own thoughts and I know mine were back in the priest hole with Donald Dhu, hoping, wishing, that his arm was all right and that he had changed the bandage.

Pringle said quietly. "Want to tell me what happened, Don?"

"Why bother. You'd never believe it."

"Try me."

It wasn't lost on me that he was appealing to my brother as the sensible member of our trio. He wasn't asking Heather or me!

"I don't think I want to talk about it, Pringle." said my brother. "I'm not used to being called a nut or a flake."

Pringle stroked in silence. Then he said: "I came across an interesting passage in the journal. . . ." As no one encouraged him—we were all sulking—he went on. "The first MacDonald in Austwick Manor recounted a strange tale. It seemed that his daughter, Margaret, told him that two little girls had visited her in her room. She thought Princess Mary had left them to be tutored and asked for instructions as to what to do with them. But no one in the house knew anything about them. A messenger was dispatched after the Princess to inquire, but she sent back word that she had left no one behind, no one at all. A search was instituted for them in the east wing and the west wing and then in the stable block, and cautious questions were asked in the village. Men even sounded the well. Nothing. MacDonald was particularly disturbed when his daughter said the girls knew about the dungeon and told him there was a prisoner in it. He was flummoxed by her story. The household finally decided they had been visited by the ghosts of two lost children. It was the only explanation."

When Pringle finished, he looked straight at us, blinking through his thick glasses. We stared back and didn't speak. He had on an Indian sweater so thick he'd have sunk if he had fallen in. I don't know why I thought of this as he waited for us to say something. I don't know what the others were thinking.

Pringle was speaking again. "Then I found another reference to the little ghosts further on in the third journal. . . ."

"What was it?" I asked because someone had to say something.

"It was at a funeral held for their heir of that particular time. It was reported that those same mysterious children attended the services. Their signatures were found in the guest book set out for the occasion. The lady of the house was writing her thank-you letters for all the condolences she'd received and found the two names last in the list. She didn't recognize them, even when her maid described them. So she made further inquiries and found a cousin's family who had seen them —he and his boy, Angus. Then there was a woman of the village employed as a mourner who spoke to them and others of her kind remembered them also. Suddenly it was all around the county that the child ghosts had been seen again. People remembered talk of the first visitation years before, just as they remembered about the curse laid on the family away back in the last century."

Don said quietly, "Does Father know this?"

"Oh yes. They saw the transcription and your mother had to type it up. Why do you think she's so upset?"

This was a new angle on things! I couldn't fit it in at once. I had to think it through. Then why this trip? Wasn't this proof enough for them? Would they believe it now? I doubted it, because they didn't wish to!

"Did these ghost children have names?" I asked shakily.

"Yes, their marks were in the guest book, remember. And Margaret MacDonald had named them, and the boy, Angus. They were the ghosts of family children, it was said, long gone—dressed strangely. No one could describe the way they were dressed—no white draperies or anything like that, everyone agreed on that. But still they couldn't describe it—it was no style that had been in fashion in all their memory."

"That was us," said Heather flatly. "But there's another ghost too, Old Tom. Margaret said he came with the house. Wouldn't it have been funny if we'd met Old Tom!"

"Oh be quiet, Heather! Stick to the point! Don't confuse things! Let's all think." said Don.

A loon gave its lonely cry. A chevron of ducks flew over, heading south. We drifted on in silence. Then Pringle said, "Tell me what happened the other night."

So we told him about Donald Dhu and the Round-head soldiers and how we had tried to get back to tend his wound and how Mother had caught us. He listened carefully, questioning us on several points and he was very thoughtful.

Don muttered, "If I hadn't been there I wouldn't have believed a word of it myself."

"I've been reading on in the journals," Pringle said. "The writing is easier now and I can go faster. I found something else. It hasn't been typed up, so your mother hasn't seen it, your father, either."

"What is it?"

"Can you take it?"

"Take what?"

"Well, I know you all feel strongly about this. I don't want Hillary to have another fit right out in the middle of the lake."

"You can stuff it, Pringle!" I said.

"It was important to get back to the Manor and they stopped us," said Heather.

"I know. That's what I read in the journal."

"What did you read?" Don asked.

"That you're a ghost too, Don."

"What do you mean?"

"This young man you left in the priest hole was there for some time. He left notes. He described what happened and he described the three of you and had names for you."

"We introduced ourselves," I said. "It was only polite."

"Yes, but you went away and didn't return and as he lay nursing his wound, he got to wondering and he remembered an old story he had heard from his nurse as a lad, that the houses had been visited more than once by the ghosts of two MacDonald children. He wrote: 'But I have gone the legend one better. I have come up with three. Another, a boy of fifteen who can throw a grown man down with so great a force that he lies stunned as one bewitched . . .' Did you use your karate on him?" Don nodded. Pringle smiled. "There wasn't much more. He complained of his wound mortifying."

"Mortifying . . . ?" I said.

"Yes, infecting. His notes became erratic, confused and soon ended."

"And then?" I asked—and yet I was afraid to hear.

"The family returned when the politics of England changed and claimed their house. Years later, someone explored it, looking for the priest hole. They found it— and a skeleton wrapped in a fur cloak. And, of course, the notes on the stool beside the cot."

There was a moment of quiet. The loon cried again and a few scattered sea gulls flapped over on their way to the coast. Tears ran down Heather's face and she

117

dashed them away impatiently. I couldn't speak. Neither could Don.

"I'd have given anything to be with you," Pringle said quietly after long minutes had passed. "Can you take me, next try?"

I sniffed and blinked hard to control my voice. "I don't think it works for anyone not of the blood, Pringle. It didn't work for Mother. She kind of dared us to prove it once. But it didn't work."

"I suppose there's some strange logic in that," he said, but he was disappointed. "But it isn't fair when it's my kind of material! My special study! It doesn't seem fair at all!"

We heard the car bumping along the rutted road around the lake and knew it was the family returning with supplies. Pringle swung the prow toward our landing. But there was more to be talked out. I said quickly, "But if you believe all that, do you believe in the curse? Because I'm worried about Don!"

Pringle lifted the oars and held them up dripping as he thought about it, and we drifted forward slowly.

"I suppose it has to be considered seriously in the light of all this." Don didn't say anything. Ordinarily he would have laughed it off, but now he was very quiet.

"We don't know what to do, Pringle," I cried. "Can a curse be lifted?"

"I don't know," he said. "It's not my specialty. But I've heard about it in voodoo."

"Yes," said Heather. "But who could do it for us? Mother wouldn't like it if we went to our Sunday School teacher and asked—"

"Keep your voice down, Heather! Don't you know how voices carry across water?" We looked shoreward where Mother was crossing the wooden porch and Father was unloading supplies from the trunk of the car. He stopped a moment and waved when he saw us looking his way.

"Priests are usually called on to do it, aren't they?" I asked.

"That's exorcism."

"Is it the same thing?"

"I don't know."

"I wouldn't want to be the one to ask the local priest," said Don grimly.

"Why not? It's your problem," said Heather. "You're the heir. You inherited."

"Shut up, Heather, " I said. "This is no time to bicker. Don just meant you can't appeal to someone outside the family. The whole neighborhood would be twittering about it. It wouldn't be good for Father at the university either, and I know Mother couldn't take it."

"We'll have to give it careful thought," said Pringle and began to row again. "I'm a student of Elizabethan England, its politics and mores, not its curses."

We rowed back in silence, our worries punctuated by the clunk of the oarlocks.

Father hailed us cheerfully, fed us a big meal, made us sing around a roaring fire afterwards and toast marshmallows, then he sent us off to bed, as he thought, tired with a healthy outdoorsy tiredness that would make us sleep dreamlessly.

CHAPTER NINE

WE WERE BACK IN TOWN EARLY TUESDAY MORNING ready for school. Each of us clutched an excuse that didn't say much. As we walked down the block, I said to Heather, "I suppose you noticed that the dolls were gone again?"

"I noticed," she said. "They were gone and they didn't put any others in their place this time. The house is empty. What do you suppose happens when there are no dolls in it?"

"It waits," I said.

Well, we were waiting, too! None of us knew what for. Something to happen to Don? I hated the waiting. If the family knew, as Pringle said they did, about the child ghosts mentioned by so many occupants of the house over the years, didn't they believe it, too?—and more important, believe in the curse? I wished I could have asked them right out but I knew they'd never admit it. Was my mother terrified and hiding it? I knew that Father, when he wasn't putting on a cheerful act, looked pretty grim. I had come into the room quietly and caught him with his face lined with worry, which immediately smoothed out to a smile when I spoke.

Don, however, threw himself into all his school

activities the first day back. I suspected he was depressed but he wouldn't talk. In addition, Father was again asking him to choke off Charlie, for he was still hanging around.

As we returned from school, we saw Charlie in his candy-apple job charge up to our house and Don hop out with only a brief wave of the hand for thanks as he crossed to the house. Charlie looked after him. I couldn't see his expression because he wore a peaked cap on his dark, curly hair and big sunglasses, but I wondered why he watched my brother the way he did as he went through our gate and up the steps. Just as we were catching up, he suddenly stepped on the gas and took off, his tires kicking up twin plumes of dust that drifted down the road to us.

"I wish Don wouldn't always ride home with him," I said.

"Why not? It would be a long walk and Don is always running late. A ride's a ride," said Heather.

"But Father doesn't like it."

"Father worries too much. Nobody bosses Don. Don is the one who influences other people."

I looked at my little sister. She always surprised me. She was right, I suppose. Who knows, Don might even change Charlie from a spoiled brat to something more human and lovable, but I doubted it. From what I heard, nobody liked him. Only my brother felt sorry for him. I left off thinking about Charlie and his car with its twenty-two coats of lacquer, because Pringle had come out of our front door to meet Don, and they now stood on the porch talking. When Pringle had said his piece, they went in. Neither one had smiled, I noticed.

"Come on," I said. "Something's up!" and I began to run the rest of the distance with Heather following, her bookbag bouncing on her back.

In the house, we found Pringle already sitting in his place at the dining table with the research all around him, and a pencil in his hand. He had been working on the journals again. Don sat at the other end saying nothing—doing nothing. He just sat with a strange, vacant expression on his face, his hands in his lap. When we came in he looked up. "Father has taken Mother to the hospital," he said.

"Is it time?" I asked in surprise.

"Early—but not too early, I think. Perhaps it was the long ride to the lake that did it."

We joined them at the table. We all sat in silence thinking of Mother and the baby who was to be called Rebecca.

"What are you doing here, Pringle?" Don asked after a long silence.

"Your father called me from the hospital and asked me to come over."

"We don't need a baby-sitter," said Don looking him in the eye. "I'm perfectly capable."

"He thought I might be able to cook you a decent meal."

"Oh well . . ." said Don. "We could have made out."

"Sure," Pringle agreed easily. "I told him that."

We sat around awhile longer until I decided I was hungry and got up to get some milk. Pringle went back to his transcribing and Don continued to just sit. None of us could voice our worry.

We were all facing the model, but only because—well, there it was. After a minute or two, Don suddenly got up and pulled out the deep drawer in the base and stared down at the dolls.

"You're not to touch them!" Heather said.

"They're mine and I'll touch them if I please," Don reminded her, and he began to lift out the first layer, the Margaret doll and the rest. Then he took out the next layer which had the lady doll in the black dress and veil. Then he looked down at Donald Dhu. I think his hand shook a little as he laid him aside carefully with his people. He was left looking at the last layer and we gathered around and stared into the drawer with him.

There was the usual set of servants, then four child dolls, a mother and father, and surprisingly, a black-robed priest. Their clothes were all different from the last lot, rich, but not with as many ribbons and bows.

"What are you going to do?"

"Set them up. We might never get another chance."

He unlocked the house and began to put the dolls in place, the cook in the kitchen, the maid on the staircase, the lady in the great chamber with her wigged husband, the children in the small chamber with their nurse. He looked at the last one, dressed all in black except for the flash of white at the neck. "Where shall we put him?"

"The chapel?"

Don placed him on a chair in the chapel, where he sat with his doll legs straight out before him and his stiff arms at his side. Then he carefully closed and locked the house once more.

"That's the last row of dolls—and that's interesting,

too." he said thoughtfully. "Why didn't the later owners of the model keep it up?—supply new figures for each successive age?"

"The journals might say something about it when we get that far along with them," said Pringle.

"What are you going to do, Don?" I asked.

"Go back in tonight."

"Then so are we!"

Pringle said nothing but blinked at us and looked worried and very envious. We were sorry about that. He might have been a help.

In the evening Father called from the hospital to say that Mother was all right but Rebecca was taking her time about arriving. He wanted to know how we were making out. Had we eaten? Had we done our homework? He said not to worry and he would call us when he had more news.

At midnight, we assembled again in the dining room. Don looked grim and determined. Pringle stood back, looking terribly out of it. The three of us joined hands. We walked toward the Tudor house and the rug turned into turf and the turf into gravel.

The scene was changed again, I noticed. The moat was filled in and the stone bridge now spanned nothing but grass. Some very large trees were missing and there were orderly flower beds laid out in patterns, but the driveway remained in the same place. And so we advanced between the beds of bright color. Don, however, didn't head for the front door but led us to the chapel end of the house.

We entered it through the small arched door and looked around. It was chill and smelled of burned-down candles and smoke and damp. Sitting where Don had put him was a priest. He had his head leaning on his hand, his elbow on the arm of the carved oak chair, and he seemed lost in thought. We watched him for a minute and then walked quietly down the short main aisle. He raised his head and looked at us. He was a youngish man, very studious-looking, with a long face like a thoughtful sheep, and now he smiled and sat up briskly.

"I can put a name to you!" he cried. We waited in some surprise. "Heather and Hillary—although I don't know which is which—and Donald!"

"I am Hillary," I said and smiled. "How do you come to know us?"

"You are the famous ghost children that go with Austwick Manor!"

"Oh no. Old Tom goes with the house. He was here the first time we visited. Margaret told us about him."

"And he hasn't been around since," said the priest. "He was an old humbug, howling and rattling his chains, I understand—so unbelievable!"

"We don't know who you are, Father." said Don.

"I am Father Francis. I'm a MacDonald too. I happen to be the brother to the MacDonald of this house."

"Why do you call us ghost children?"

"Ah . . . ! I know all about you! I'm extremely interested in such things! I've studied the old journals and diaries and I know of every appearance you have made! May I say I'm extremely honored that you have visited me? What can I do to serve you? You must have come for a reason."

"Have you heard about the Curse of the Seer?"

"Indeed I have—to the family's sorrow."

"Do you believe in it?"

"Unfortunately, it is well documented."

"This is my brother. He is the heir in a second generation. We're afraid for him and want to prevent anything happening to him. We've already lost our father."

"Ah . . . ! But wait. I'm sorely puzzled. Where do you fit in? Sometime before the unfortunate girl Margaret, who died a bride in Spain, perhaps?—because you did appear to her. It's recorded in the journal. I don't quite understand how this can be."

Don said gently. "We're MacDonalds from the future, Father."

The priest's face lit up. "You mean you haven't been born yet?"

"Oh yes, we've been born, but in a future time."

He rubbed his hands together delightedly. "This *is* a privilege! My goodness! To think this is happening to me!"

"Could you help us?" I asked because I was anxious about our problem. "If we can't get help to cancel out the curse, Don might . . . well, you know. The family might come to an end."

Father Francis sobered at once and looked at Don. "It's so wicked—unthinkable—but what do you suggest?"

"Couldn't the curse be canceled out?" said Don. "What about exorcising it? Couldn't you do that?"

The priest cocked his head on one side and thought about it. He had the high, arched nose and the bright blue eye of all the MacDonalds. "He was a powerful rascal and made a powerful curse," he said. "A dreadful man, and evil! The question is: was he foretelling the misfortunes of poor Mary Tudor or was he laying a curse on her? Whichever it was, he proved a dangerous

126

man. I don't blame the MacDonald for locking him up."

"But the exorcism?"

"You must know some suitable words more powerful even than that old man's black magic," insisted Heather.

Father Francis looked nervous and pulled his long upper lip. "For something like this I should consult my bishop," he said. "Yes, definitely. But how can I without him concluding I'm quite mad? 'Do an exorcism for three ghost children of Austwick Manor?' he'd say. 'If you'd even pretended it was for the benefit of the present family! But for ghost children, you say? Better exorcise them while you're at it.' No, no, Donald, I cannot put such an extraordinary proposition to him!"

"If you don't, I'm very likely the last of the line," Don said.

"What, you have no younger brothers to inherit?"

"Only a cousin somewhere who is a traveling musician of some kind. He's not in the direct line."

"No, and he doesn't sound the right kind at all. Well, it seems I have a choice of being thought mad by my superior or contributing to the final extinction of this noble house, which is, after all, my own."

He was dithering and it made me more anxious still. I said, "Good! You've decided! Now let's hurry, Father, because we're very worried and concerned. . . ."

It worked. He said, "Then, let's go to the library and consult some of the books. Come." He jumped up suddenly and we followed his flapping skirts down the aisle, and all our feet made shushing noises on the stone floor.

In the front hall, we passed a lady with a pretty

yellow dress and beauty marks on her face and her hair piled high. Heather stared. One tiny black patch was in the shape of a new moon, and two others were little stars. She smiled and said, "More catechism classes, Francis? Afterwards, give your friends some apples to take home. We have a good crop this year."

"By all means, Louise. I'll do that. We're on our way to the library now."

The lady went into the great hall and closed the door. Father Francis chuckled. "Won't she be surprised when I tell her someday!" he said. Still chuckling, he led us to the east wing and down a hall, threw open a door, and we entered the library. Here the books were shelved from floor to ceiling, and there was a small balcony running around high up and a circular stairway in the corner where you could climb up to it and consult the books near the ceiling. We stood and looked around and I thought how excited Father would be to see it—and Pringle. Don nudged me. I looked and saw a shelf of books that I recognized, our journals and daily account books beginning with the first one of 1540! They didn't look as battered and rotting as they did now, resting in their raw-wood packing cases in Don's room at home— and, of course, we had more of them. But Father Francis did not reach for one of these, but for a small book, a kind of diary, with heavy metal clasps, which had not come down to us.

"This," he said almost gleefully, "is a very private little book kept under lock and key by the first MacDonald and carried on by a son, Rory."

"One of the twins!" I cried.

"You know?" Father Francis said, delighted.

"We have the journals. The first MacDonald had a

daughter Margaret, an heir Donald, and twins, Rory and Ian."

"Excellent! Oh, how exciting this is! Well now," he said and sobered quickly, "the curse caught up with the MacDonald and his heir. The next son Rory tells us how their deaths came about. The MacDonald was killed when a ship he was sailing in was wrecked on the way to the Low Countries, and his heir was killed en route to join an expedition to Ireland. Fortunately there were the twins to carry on. We are descended from them."

We must all have been thinking the same thing, that that was the first time the curse had struck down the head of the family and his heir before their time! Father Francis was opening the old diary and he turned swiftly to a certain place and began tracing the heavy Elizabethan script with a bony finger and reading it off. Pringle would have been impressed, I thought.

"Rory's writing begins where his father's leaves off and it had to do with the man in the dungeon. Let's see what he says." He began to read.

> "In as much as my esteemed father left us this fortnight past and took ship with a sea captain called Quiller, a villainously scarred ship's master with the mark of the devil on his countenance, and in as much as my older brother had already met his end with a hard-driving whip who was engaged to coach him to Bristol, he, my father, thought it wise to leave in our hands the care of his household, my lady mother being much grieved for her son, besides not being conversant with all problems therein. He

had particular and secret instructions for us in connection with an erstwhile prisoner of his, one Rankard Izard, or some such name, who, because of his vilification of Her Royal Highness our late Queen Mary, he thought best to put where he could do least damage with his dire foretellings and forebodings the likes of which made man sick who didst hear him speak it. My brother and myself were, therefore, informed of all things therein. Our man, Leadbettor, being his sole keeper was seeing to the care and feeding and well-being of this infamous prattler of prophesies, for he must be kept in good health withal so that the threats he made against this house come not about. So said our sire to us.

"These instructions we have well and faithfully carried out—our servant Leadbettor also—but the rascal below, having attained a hoary age, did die despite all care. The disposal of his body did much trouble us, but on consultation with my brother and the keeper, we concluded to bury the miscreant where he lay and have done with it, anywhere else causing talk in the village which would not be good withall. And so it was done and neatly by the light of our lanthorn, and by it, his gray locks looked like bleached snakes and the mark of the cloven hoof on his forehead did stand out livid on the whiteness of his face and in the dimness I thought his eye did lose its glaze and glitter strongly.

We were glad to see him safely under Lead-
bettor's stone and mortar for all time and an
end to him. We then adjourned to the chapel
where we said a prayer of thanksgiving for
being free of the villain at last."

Father Francis removed his pale, bony finger from beneath the line of script. Heather was looking round-eyed and I shivered in spite of myself. It was Don who spoke first.

"So he's down there still!"

"What's left of him," said Father Francis. "We must find the remains. Yes, that's the first thing to do."

"Will that take long?" I asked.

"Everything takes time—but Rory has told us where they put him and it's a very small space. I've been down there."

But Don was worried. He didn't know how much time we had. One night? When our parents were back in the house we might never have another chance! They would see to that. So we watched Father Francis fuss. He moved jerkily, impulsively—but never seemed to get much done and we became anxious. He clearly needed a firm hand.

"Let me help, Father. What are we looking for?" I said.

He looked around vaguely, darting here and there among the bookshelves. After discarding many, he finally found the ones he wanted and I collected them and passed some to the others to carry.

"Are we going to need any tools? Don asked.

"Tools!" Father Francis exclaimed. "Certainly tools!" and he scuttled from the library. We followed with the books. He led us back into the front of the house and through to the kitchen. Both Don and Heather had been there when we tried to help Donald Dhu, but I had not. Now I stared over my load of musty leather bindings at the cavern of a fireplace, at the walls covered with copper pans and large dish covers and the dressers lined with crockery. The cook was rolling out pastry, her arms floured to the elbows, a dab on her nose. She looked up as we hurried through, but Father Francis ignored her and went to a door in the paneling of one wall and pushed. He found a candle on a nearby shelf and lit it. From its feeble glow, we saw a stone staircase beyond, very like the circular one that led from the chapel into the crypt, and he disappeared down it like a rabbit down a hole, only to pop up again and shout sternly, "We don't wish to be disturbed, Cook! That's an order!" The woman stared in silence, then turned back to her baking. I had the feeling that she was used to Father Francis's eccentricities.

"Shut the door!" he called up, and I obeyed, kicking it shut as best I could with my arms full, then I moved down after the others, feeling each narrow step with a cautious toe before coming down on it or else I might have pitched down with my load.

We had descended into a stone cellar of many arches. By the candle I dimly made out kegs, barrels and racks of bottles in the cool recesses of the foundations. There was a workbench against one wall and Father Francis found two lanterns there and lit them. Then he chose a broad chisel and a large hammer. He pushed one lantern at Don, held the other high himself and said, "Come!"

CHAPTER TEN

WE FOLLOWED HIS FLAPPING SKIRTS ONCE MORE AND
he led us across to a small, almost invisible door behind a
giant barrel. He took down a great key from a nail, put it
in the lock and began to struggle with it. Don finally
said, "Let me, Father," and with a strong twist, turned
it over. He pushed the small door with his shoulder and
the musty, foul air seemed to rush out and envelope us.

The dungeon was about eight feet square. The
frame of the cot was still in place, also the iron basket
that was the brazier and the two buckets. There was a
slit of a window high up in the outside wall, which laid
a band of bright light on the opposite stone wall. The
floor was the same as that of the wine cellar outside,
large squares of slate.

"Now where is he?"

We dropped all the books on the wooden frame of
the cot and now we stood and looked around the dungeon. I was nervous. We had pushed Father Francis to
this point but now I didn't know if I could go through
with it! I had a feeling that someone would creep across
the cellar and slam the door on us. I looked at Heather.
She must be feeling it worse. I expected to feel her hand

133

searching for mine, but she was staring down at a large slab in the middle of the space.

"He's under there," she said pointing.

At the sound of her voice heard for the first time, Father Francis looked startled and turned to Don. "Your sister is fey?" he whispered. Then he shook his head and said, "I keep forgetting that you are ghosts! Why shouldn't she know!"

"She's just guessing," Don said.

"I am not. He's under that stone right there."

Father Francis promptly seized the broad chisel and the hammer and got down on the dungeon floor and began to chip away at the mortar. The blows rang out sharply on the chisel and echoed around the stone walls. I wondered if it could be heard upstairs. Don must have thought the same, for he closed the stout oak door. But I wished he hadn't closed it! I tried not to panic!

"Light! Light! More light!" called Father Francis, and we hurried to hold the lanterns over him while he worked.

His arm quickly tired and Don took over and chipped around the square with speed. Soon it was free and we looked at each other nervously.

"You girls had better wait outside," Don said quietly.

"Not I," said Heather.

I would have gone, but now I couldn't, and they took it that we were in agreement for staying, so Don inserted the chisel under one corner of the slab and lifted and levered it sideways until they could haul it across its neighboring stone. Immediately a strong, earthy smell filled our nostrils—the smell of earth without benefit of sunlight or rain. It choked us and made

134

us cough. I don't know if we were expecting a cavity under the stone but there wasn't one. Only the dusty dry rubble that made us gasp.

Don muttered, "You'd better be right, Heather, because now we have to dig. We could be here all night and find nothing."

"I'm right," she said.

Don looked irritated but determined. "We need a spade," he said.

Father Francis scuttled out to look for one. Again I had the overpowering fear of being left—of someone slamming the door and turning the big key and leaving us until the lanterns burned out and we were abandoned in the dark. I dug my nails into my palms to stop from bolting.

While he was gone, Don impatiently seized the chisel and with the hammer, pounded it down into the rubble. It sank under his blows fairly easily, proving I hoped, that the earth had at one time been disturbed and repacked and that we were in the right place. Suddenly it met a slight resistance and he stopped.

Father Francis appeared with a spade and a trowel and they both dug, getting in each other's way and tossing debris out over our feet. We coughed and sneezed and rubbed our eyes. When they got down about a foot —and with the chisel still standing upright in the middle of the space and the earth now gone around it—they threw aside their tools and began to scoop out earth with their bare hands.

"The chisel hit something, I know it did!" gasped Don.

Only their breathing and coughing and the tinkle of small pebbles on stone as they tossed them aside into the dark beyond the circle of light broke the heavy silence. Heather and I knelt at the hole and held the lanterns high. They smoked, and the dry earth-smell combined with it to make us all constantly clear our throats. Once I glanced up to see our shadows dancing eerily on the walls and I looked away quickly.

They both uncovered a flash of white bone at the same time.

"I told you! Didn't I tell you?" cried Heather.

No one answered her as a skull was cleared of earth. It grinned up at us horribly. Everyone drew back and stared and in the flickering shadows, it seemed to stare back. Father Francis set about uncovering the skeleton's arms, which seemed to be held stiffly before it, the clenched hands almost under its clenched jaw. The chisel had entered the hole at the top of the skull and pinned it to the earth below, but the front was intact and its eye sockets were clogged with dirt and its jaw appeared studded with black and broken teeth. There was a tuft of something white which might have been his hair or some strange filament from which mush-rooms grew. I shivered. It seemed more sinister than the earth-stained bones.

Father Francis murmured, "He's been there for over a century! It's hard to believe he's still dispensing evil."

"A century to your time, Father, but almost four centuries to ours," Don reminded him.

"My, my!" he said and then looked across at Heather and me still holding the lanterns. "But I feel this is distressing your sisters."

"Our museum at home is full of old bones," said

Heather. "Mostly animal bones. I don't mind. I'm going to be a doctor."

"Fancy that!" he said. He turned back to the hole then and began to mutter a prayer for the dead. We were silent, listening.

In the middle of a sentence, when he was asking a gentle forgiveness, he stopped and suddenly cried, "Look!"

It jerked us all to attention. He seized my hand holding the lantern and moved it to the left. "Look!" he said again. "That mark on the temple bone! The mark of the cloven hoof! It's the mark of the devil! The devil has put his mark on him for all time!"

We peered down into the hole. It wasn't quite a horseshoe, having a break in the lowest curve and it did look like a cloven hoof.

Father Francis was now very excited. "Remember what Rory said about the death of his father from a villainous captain? The man's face was marked by a curious scar, he said. And the son and heir?—killed by a murderous coachman, a man 'scarred with the mark of Satan.' "

I said shakily, "And Donald Dhu's Roundhead soldier had a similar mark on his temple. I thought he had hit his head on the chest when you threw him—remember, Don?"

My brother was looking thoughtful. "I seem to have seen a scar like that before. . . ." he said.

Father Francis went on excitedly. "Family history says that the heir who died in 1625 was killed by a highwayman with just such a scar and his father was led into a Yorkshire bog by a villainous guide, marked, so the locals said, 'as if a goat had kicked him.' "

137

There was a mark on the face of the doll that was the seer—and I'd thought it just a rust mark on the old linen!

At that moment, Father Francis freed the lantern and as I recovered the swaying light, I saw a glint among the bones. "There's something in his hand," I whispered and pointed.

Don reached down and moved the hands, which were clasped together, and whatever it was fell away from the cage of bones that were the fingers. He picked it up. It was a small figure carved from an amethyst crystal. Only the head and body were in the clear purple part of the stone; the cloven hooves were carved in the brown base rock from which the crystal had grown; the horns on its head were carved in the dirty gray tip. But the eyes!—they were clear and bulbous and highly polished. Don turned it in the palm of his hand. It was loathsome.

Father Francis gasped and cried, "Diabolus!" He stumbled to his feet and rushed to his books. "Light! Light!" he cried. I quickly brought my lantern to where he searched for the book he wanted. "We must destroy it at once! We have searched out the evil, and it must be destroyed! Destroyed forever!" He found the page and began to read quickly, facing Don where he crouched holding the tiny figure. "I abjure thee, Satan! Leave this place! I abjure thee Lucifer! I rebuke thee! All heaven rebukes thee! . . . Destroy it!" he shouted at Don. "Destroy it now, I say! . . . Hail, Jesus Christ. Hail, God of Abraham, hail, God of Isaac, hail, God of Jacob, Holy Ghost, Son of the Father, who's among the Seven of the Seven. As above! As below! I invoke thee all! Destroy the evil one! The malignant one! Destroy!"

"Destroy it!" I shouted to Don. I wanted to rush to him where he crouched with Heather staring down at the thing in his hand. He seemed paralyzed, unable to move. But Father Francis needed the light, and I was anchored to him and his incantation. "Destroy it!" I shouted again across the space. "Smash it and save yourself!"

Don moved. He laid the figure on the raised slab and picked up the hammer. Suddenly a wind arose. It whistled through the high slit in the outside wall and swirled around us. It lifted our hair, flapped the father's robes and formed eddies in the dry earth that arose and blinded us. There was a wailing sound that came with it, first a great shushing, then a strange whistling. And it was cold! It was so cold that we shook with it. My teeth chattered and the lantern in my hand swung and I could not steady it.

Don had trouble leaning against the wind, but he braced himself with one foot planted on the other rim of the hole. He lifted the hammer and brought it down squarely on the figure. It splintered like glass. The house shook. The timbers above our heads moved. The iron brazier went over with a clatter. The wind screamed and swept dust into his eyes. Blindly, he brought the hammer down again, and this time the gem stone pulverized into a gray powder and the wind died with a terrible sobbing scream.

Father Francis fell back across the cot and brought up against the stone wall in the darkness beyond the circle of my light, the leaves of his book flapped wildly. I sank down beside him and leaned against the wooden frame. Heather and Don clung to each other. Their lantern had fallen into the hole among the bones and now glowed up from below, throwing a square of pale light on the beams above. Gradually they both sagged back against the piles of earth that had been thrown out and just lay there panting.

The stillness was eerie. I closed my eyes and heard echoing in my ears, Father Francis's words over and over again, "Go forth! I abjure thee! I abjure thee!"

CHAPTER ELEVEN

THERE WAS A DISTANT POUNDING THAT CAME CLOSER and closer until my head felt ready to burst. I covered my ears and opened my eyes a slit. Our bedroom door was ajar and Don and Pringle were beating a tattoo on it. They were both grinning broadly.

"Rebecca has arrived!" they announced.

Heather sat up and blinked. "Rebecca?"

"Yes! Rebecca!"

"Father called! Mother is fine!"

"He'll be home soon!" Pringle said.

I looked at my brother. My anxiety took shape. The events of last night flooded over me. Now I remembered the black dungeon and the howling wind and the choking stench of dry dust and the house shaking above us and Father Francis's words riding above the wind. Don seemed lighter somehow—happier. I hadn't seen him look quite so carefree for a long time. I said shakily, remembering it all, "Don?"

He said quickly, "It's all right, Hillary!" He smiled just for me. "It's all right. I've told Pringle what happened, and we've removed all the dolls."

"I'd have given anything to have been there!" Pringle said. "It was so weird. You started to fade away and then—well, then you were gone! I guess I fell asleep waiting. I woke up this morning and you were already back and asleep."

"Well, I'm hungry now," Don cried. "I'm ravenous! Get up and let's eat!" They left and thundered down the stairs to the kitchen. I marveled at how my brother had thrown it all off! His spirits had bobbed up like a cork. Only now did I fully realize how worried he had been.

We showered and got dressed. As we pulled on our clothes, I remembered something else that had been bothering me. I said, "Heather, how did you know for sure he was buried under that middle stone?"

She shrugged. "Common sense. Three people buried him. Rory, his twin brother, Ian, and the keeper. Think of it. It was such a small space there wouldn't have been room for them all to work at once on one of the stones nearer the wall without getting in each other's way— and they were eager to have done with it. Rory's own words. 'Have done with it.' It had to be the one out in the clear."

Simple!

We went down to the kitchen where Don and Pringle were still in high spirits. It was easy to see that Don felt as if the world had been lifted off his shoulders, and suddenly we felt the same. We shouted at each other happily and laughed at things that were too silly to describe. Everything made us laugh. The shape of a fried egg, spilled milk and burned toast. We rolled with laughter and couldn't stop and our jaws ached with it. And each time we stopped, something—a look, a hic-cough—would start us off again. And Pringle laughed as hard as any of us.

Then Father came home. He looked relieved and

happier, but a little serious, too. We talked of Rebecca, who weighed in at seven pounds and was, he said, "very pink," and of Mother, who was very happy. Then he turned to Don and looked strangely solemn. "Don, have you listened to the news this morning?"

"No. Why?"

"There's been a bad accident."

Don said suddenly, "Charlie?"

Father was surprised and so were the rest of us. We wondered why Don had jumped to such a conclusion.

"Yes," Father said. "An accident in his car—sometime after midnight—he must have lost control. He hit a pole and the gas tank exploded. The police say there's not enough left to examine and come to any conclusion." Don's gaze seemed far away. "I'm sorry," said Father. "While your mother and I didn't like anything we heard about Charlie, we couldn't wish such an end as this on anybody. Thank God you weren't with him this time!"

No one spoke. Father arose slowly. "Well," he said, "I'll get ready for work. I ate in the hospital cafeteria." He threw a last look of concern at Don, who was still sitting quietly at the table, and went upstairs to change.

We sat on. I glanced at my brother uneasily. I didn't know anything about Charlie would affect him so deeply.

"I'm sorry, Don," I said.

He looked up from his plate. "You remember all that talk of Father Francis's about the mark of Satan that comes right down through history? Charlie had it. He hid it with his cap."

We stared at him. "You mean Charlie was the one this time around?—like the ship's captain and the coachman and the Roundhead soldier?"

"And the highwayman who killed an heir on his way home from London and the guide who led the father into a Yorkshire bog?"

We sat quietly, everyone marveling over it, but I was struck with an uncomfortable question: Who was the stranger who had met up with our own father years ago? Could it have been the man who rented him the rowboat that morning? He must have been the last person our father saw that day unless, sometime later perhaps, a fast speedboat sideswiped him and tipped him out. We would never know.

I was brought back to the present by the sound of a light step and a faint smell of shaving lotion as Father, newly shaved, came through the kitchen again.

"You may telephone the hospital and speak to your mother now. She'll be awake. Pringle, you have classes this morning?"

Pringle arose. "Yes, sir. I have." He blinked around at us and his eyes touched on the model of Austwick Manor.

"Come on. I'll give you a lift," said Father. "I rather hesitated to ask you to stay over, so I'm glad you enjoyed yourself."

"Be seeing you, Pringle," we called. "And thank you."

"Anytime," he answered solemnly. "Just ask me anytime!"